Sula & Ja

Ellen Banda-Aaku

Gadsden Publishers

Gadsden Publishers
PO Box 32581, Lusaka, Zambia

First published in 2015 for East Africa by Storymoja, Kenya
This edition published in 2015 for Southern Africa

ISBN: 978-9982-24-100-7

Printed by Lightening Source UK Ltd

Chapter 1

Sula

You would have thought that after a whole year of being paired with Ja Maponya in Science and ICT I would be used to it. No chance. He's standing close to me tapping his foot and humming some rap song as we wait for the iodine in the test tube I'm holding to react. Sweat is trickling down the sides of my body and settling in wet patches in the waistband of my black school skirt. And no matter how hard I try to steady it, my hand just won't stop shaking.

'Shouldn't you be writing?' I ask. At least my voice is steady.

'All written, madam.' Ja scribbles something down and smacks the Biro onto the notepad. He has this irritating habit of calling me madam. I pretend not to mind. Reacting to it will encourage him.

The bells ring and the lab erupts, chairs screech across the floor, water taps gush as lab apparatuses are washed and everyone seems to start talking at once. Brother Paul our Science teacher shouts above the noise that the lab should be cleaned up before we leave.

Ja starts cleaning out the test tubes while I go through what he's written in the chart. When his back is turned I dot one of his I's and pencil over the number 5 which looks like the letter S.

I write a few additional points in the columns, then ask if what I've written is okay. As if I don't know it is. Brother Paul paired Ja and me because we are the top science students in the entire school, so I really don't need Ja to verify my work.

'Perfect madam,' he says, and I wish I could punch him in the face. If I did, it would wipe the stupid smile off his face but I would get kicked out of school and lose the scholarship I was granted last month to study at a university in the United States. If that happened, my mother who I call Amai and her twin sister Amai Mukulu will have nothing to say to their customers. The two sisters run a tailoring business from home and for the last month all their poor customers have heard is, 'Our Sula is going to study in America.'

'Hey Ja, you done?' Tiger, one of Ja's friends or rather followers shunts over to us. 'Let's go man.' He gestures with his head for Ja to follow him, then hesitates and looks at me. Tiger, fair skinned, with zillions of pimples dotted on his face; Leopard would have been a more suitable nickname for him than Tiger. But his father is supposedly one of the richest men in the country so no one seems to notice the pimples. I can tell from the way Tiger eyes me that he's going to say something horrible. I brace myself.

'So are you going to the dance?' he asks. Two other members of the gang Maposha and Raymond have joined us. They all look at me as if I'm of a different species, a species; that does not awe them but one that is handy enough as an object for light entertainment when there's nothing better to do.

I ignore them all. I start packing my bag. But when I reach for the notepad and file Ja does the same. 'I'll take it.' He gets to it first.

'It's due on Monday. I have to do the write-up.' I manage not to sound as panicky as I feel. I know he's capable of doing the write-up but the only way I can feel assured that it's done well is if I do it myself.

'I got it,' he says. 'I will do the write-up this time.'

We face one another. Lucy, Ja's apparent girlfriend and Kenya, Tiger's girlfriend and Liseli, another female member of their gang walk over and form a semicircle around Ja and me. I feel like a hare, cornered. My heartbeat starts to quicken, my stomach churns. I feel myself shrinking.

'It's okay, I'll do it,' I say trying hard to suppress my panic.

'You've done it the last four times. We're meant to be working together, partners remember!' Ja says.

I let go of the folder because I suddenly need some fresh air. I pick up my pencil case and folder, hoist my bag on my shoulder. I am grateful that Amai Mukulu recently bought me a bag at the second-hand market in town. Then I remember the other notes I have on the usb and rummage around in the bottom of my bag. They are all watching me. I try to think of something to say to break the silence, to stop them from staring. If only I was Joyce, my elder sister, *always with a razor sharp word in her mouth and defecates everywhere*, as Bambo my father often says of her. Because if I were Joyce I would surely have a sassy parting shot for this bunch of dimwits. Something that would make them stay away from me.

But I am only Sula, so I hand over the usb and hear myself say, 'Ja, please make sure you do it by Monday.'

'Trust me, madam,' Ja says, and his friends chuckle in a chorus.

Tiger, who has undone his red school tie and tied it around his forehead like a bandana, snatches the usb from Ja and reads the label taped to it. 'Sula and Ja?' He looks me over and scoffs. I feel my face burn. The girls close in on Tiger to read what's written on the usb. 'Ooh cosy,' Tiger says, moving his mouth dramatically. 'Suuulala and Jaaaa!' The girls burst out laughing.

As I turn away, Ja snatches the usb back. I hear them scuffling around, but I don't turn back. Then Kenya comes after me and asks, 'Sula, are you coming to the dance?' She doesn't ask because she is interested in my answer. Since I came to the school

I am always asked questions to remind me I don't belong. Questions such as: *Sula, where do you live? Sula, where does your father work? Sula, what school did you say you were at before you came to St Mathews?*

I turn around and announce to Kenya that I am not going to the dance. I get ready to tell her that my reasons are none of her business, but Raymond interjects at that moment: 'Oh, is it because you don't have a partner?' and covers his mouth as if he has said something he shouldn't have.

Tiger butts in, 'Oh, but she does have a partner. Ja, remember it's Suuulala and Jaaaa!' They all laugh out loud as Ja tells Tiger to grow up.

I glare at him. I try to get away, but the handle on my schoolbag keeps sliding off my shoulder, making it awkward for me to sashay off. As I make to tighten the handle, I hear Tiger say, 'Ja, I think Suuuulala wants to be your partner at the dance.'

'Go on then, Ja. Ask the lady out?' Maposha prompts Ja.

Some other students have gathered around now for a laugh. Being paired with Ja who is unarguably the most popular boy in the school has made me a magnet for cruel jokes and comments. No one had seemed to care much about me when I arrived at the school and they discovered I didn't belong. They ignored me and so I was able to mind my own business in peace. But in the second year Brother Paul paired me with Ja for our science classes. For all he cared, I might as well have been a lab specimen with a label screaming: *Hate me!*

If the truth be known, I have been dreading the school leaver's dance since I arrived at St Matthews. I knew I couldn't attend because I hate dancing and loud music, Bambo would not allow me out at night, I have choir practice on Friday evenings and I am a soloist so I have to go, etc., etc. Those were the excuses I had already lined up in my head for this moment because I knew I would be asked eventually if I was going to the dance. Though the real reasons are: I don't have any friends at school, and I don't have a pretty dress to wear.

Suddenly, I feel a surge of anger at Kenya for asking. But I don't show it. My strategy towards the students over the past two years has been to stay aloof - from everyone - at school, just as Joyce had advised. She said, 'Don't let them know you're from Bellington Girls High or that you live in Bellington or worse still that your school fees are not being paid by Bambo but by his ex-boss Mr Jan Helgesen.' And when I asked how I could keep such information secret without it eventually coming to light, Joyce had replied, 'Simple; just don't make friends with them. Go to school, do your work, come back home. If you don't talk to anyone of them how will they find out?'

Now they are using the dance to show me up. I can tell from the smiles on their faces that they are enjoying the show. They know that there is no way Ja would invite me to the dance because Ja can take anyone he wants to the dance, so why would he pick poor simple Sula from Bellington? He has top grades in class, he has won school senior sports boy of the year twice, he is Deputy Head Boy although rumour has it that he was favoured because his mother donated a mini-bus to the school, and he sings and plays the guitar very well. So with such fine credentials why he would invite me, the girl from Bellington, to the dance?

As I walk away, I hear Tiger say, 'Did you just turn her down?' Then I hear him cluck twice and say, 'Chicken,' to Ja. There's more laughter.

I hasten my pace, angry with myself for being caught off guard. I didn't expect anyone to say to my face that no one wanted to invite me. I feel my chest start to tighten. I had thought that I was strong and wouldn't let them get to me but now I realise I was wrong. I hope the tears I feel welling up will stay put at least until I am out of the school gates. I hurry down the corridor, out the building, towards the exit gate. Thank God, tomorrow is the last day of the third and final term. Study leave comes next week, followed by exams. And then I don't have to see Kenya's skinny legs and Tiger's pimply face ever again.

I dodge around the students streaming out the gates. I hear someone calling my name. It is Ja. I know it's him, but I carry on walking. Then I hear his hurried footsteps.

'Sula!'

I stop and turn to face him.

'What?'

'Will you come to the dance with me?' Ja has a smile on his face, his cheeky mouth twisted to the side. I look at him, then at Tiger and the company who have stopped a few paces away. The whole gang has followed him. I can see Ja's friends jostling one another and laughing from a distance. I know they have come along to see if Ja will call Tiger's bluff because I know it's a game of daring one another and they are using me as the toy. I wonder what is at stake. An X-box game? A pack of magic cards, or a kiss from Lucy or one of the girls? I know I must say a loud *no* for everyone to hear. But it doesn't quite come out as planned. 'Why don't you just leave me alone?' I hear myself asking him. 'What have I done to you?'

He stops smiling.

I go on: 'I don't want to go to the dance. I didn't ask to be your lab partner. Brother Paul put us together, remember? And you are the one who wrote both our names on the usb, so leave me alone!' I say it loud and confident. But as I utter my last words my voice breaks off and the tears I thought I was managing to contain fill my eyes such that Ja's face blurs before me. Angry, more at myself for crying than at Ja for being so cruel, I walk away.

He calls my name again, but I carry on walking. I hear Tiger jeer, I hear someone laughing; though I don't hear what Ja says, I am sure he tells them I am crying. And before I can stop myself I do something stupid. I break into a run.

Chapter 2

Ja

Mwati, Ma's driver, is trying to strike up a conversation about football, but I'm not in the mood. I wish he could just keep his eyes on the road and drive instead of swinging his head back and forth between the road ahead and me sitting in the back of the Highlander. I feel rotten.

Although my knee has recovered after I twisted it from playing football, and is *as good as new* as the Doctor told Ma, it feels a bit stiff at times. But I am happy to be back at school. I don't have to lie in bed counting the ceiling tiles like I recently had to do for two weeks. But what's really getting me is what happened with Sula last time. Tiger can be a jerk but then so can I. I made Sula cry for the sake of a laugh with the guys. I can't take the look on Sula's face before she ran off out of my mind. Why did Tiger have to start it all up? He has a nice side to him, if only he showed it more often.

He's always trying to pick on Sula. Granted, she can be a bit weird in that she won't talk to anyone and seems to really go out of her way to ensure she doesn't endear herself to anyone, but she didn't deserve to be made a fool of. And although Tiger later insisted he hadn't meant to make her cry, he knew he was being unkind. I only asked her to the dance because I expected her to give me one of her dagger stares and then walk away as if I didn't matter, but her tears caught me unawares. When Brother Paul paired me with Sula I protested, because I wanted to partner with one of the guys to make life much easier, but he insisted I partner with Sula. She doesn't talk much to me or anyone else. Other pairs meet up outside school to do their work but Sula and I have never had to. I know she wouldn't want to meet up with me because I get the feeling she doesn't like me. But then again she has no friends so I guess it's not about me; she probably doesn't like anyone.

I give Mwati a few responses in monosyllables and plug in my earphones. He gets the message because he switches on the car radio.

To be honest, I was half hoping I would still be off sick by the time the dance came around so I wouldn't have to decide whom to invite. It's proving to be too much hassle for an event that will only last a few hours. The fuss over whom I'll invite. Tiger and Kenya nearly drove me crazy with the texts asking if I'd be back in time for the dance and with their suggestions of who I should invite. I toyed with the idea of inviting Lucy, but the rumours that she's my girlfriend irritate me, so inviting her would only fuel the rumours. And the way she made fun of Sula who didn't do anything to her has convinced me even more that Lucy is a nasty piece of work. I have thought of Mercy, from the second form six class, only because Ma keeps dropping hints about what a nice girl Mercy is and keeps reminding me that we are good family friends, and that her mother had called to ask Ma who I was inviting. Ma said to me the other day, 'Imagine Mercy's mum called to ask who you were inviting to the dance as if it was any of her business,' though what she actually meant to say was, 'Ja please invite Mercy to the dance.' The one thing I know about Ma, mainly because she is constantly denying it, is this: anything that is my business is her business too. I am reluctant to invite Mercy; she's very pretty but every other word that comes out of her mouth is: my father this, my father that. Quite frankly I don't want to spend the evening talking about her Dad.

Considering my lack of options, I might as well go to the dance with Sula. She has been a great lab partner: I haven't done much of the work but thanks to her, I have an A+ in our coursework. I know she cried because she thought I was being mean, but if I follow through and take her to the dance then there was nothing wrong with my asking her in the first place. Spending the night by her side shouldn't be too bad; after all, I have spent four hours a week with her in the lab and that hasn't killed me. I'm sure she would make an effort to look nice. A few of the guys at school call her the U girl as in U for ugly. But I think she's more plain than ugly.

My mobile rings, just then.

Mwati turns around and mouths to me, 'Tell her we'll be home soon.'

Predictable Ma calls at exactly the same time everyday to check that I'm okay.

'Bobo, where are you? How come you're not home yet? How was school?' Ma calls me Bobo from when I was a baby. When I tell her all's well, Ma asks to speak to Mwati. I remind her that he shouldn't be talking on the phone because he's driving, but she insists. She sounds more hysterical than her usual self, so I hand over the phone.

When Mwati hangs up he says to me, 'Your mother said that I should get you home now because something has happened.' He looks worried but he always looks worried because Ma often stresses him out. I don't say anything, because Ma could be dramatic at times; it could be something as trivial as a bird poo on her windscreen, or her hair got wet.

But then something stirs in my stomach. It hasn't been a good day for me. Now I sense it's about to get worse.

When I get home I find Ma in my bedroom. I hate the way she is always in my room; it worked when I was eight but now I can't stand it and she doesn't seem to get my point. I smell the smoke on her. Ma is a closet smoker which annoys me to no end, but today I decide not to start on that one, to let it slide. I want her to get whatever it is off her mind and vacate my room.

'Bobo, Mummy needs to tell you something.' She hesitates, then says, 'I got a message today. You father is very sick.'

I feel a pull in my gut and I know that should be a guy's reaction to hearing his old man is ill. But I'm surprised at myself for feeling gutted. I haven't seen the guy in over six years. He has never really been in my life, so what does it matter? Honestly speaking, if the man died today my life would go on as usual. I look at Ma and wonder why she's looking so sad. She hates the guy. I often wonder how and why she got close enough to him to conceive me. My grandparents hate him even more. Nana and Papa always felt my father was not good enough for their precious daughter.

I remember my sixth birthday, in particular. Ma and I were still living with Nana and Papa at the time, and they had arranged a big party for me. I remember big balloons, blue and white, crisp white tablecloths, colourful wrapped gifts, and my outfit: navy blue shorts, braces and a blue bowtie with polka dots. Sometime during that afternoon Nana called me aside and led me into the house. I remember the house felt cold and dark compared to the bright sun outside. Nana led me to the smaller living-room and asked me to go inside. She stood at the door. I knew she was listening.

I found a thin man perched on the edge of a chair. He sat as if he was trying hard not to crease the chair, as if he was about to run away. I knew who he was because I had seen him on previous birthdays. He put me on his lap. I remember wondering why his legs were shaking and why he spoke in a whisper. He didn't stay long. He bounced me up and down on his lap, asked me a few questions, handed me a bright red ball before he left. But before he left he said something to me. He whispered to me that I should never forget him. He said he was my father and would always be. I was left feeling sad that day. I was sad because I saw the way Nana looked at my father as he was leaving and because I know he saw it too.

I remember asking her why she didn't like him as she walked back outside to the party. She muttered something and tried to take my ball from me so that I could go and play with my friends. But I held on tight, making sure I took it outside to show my friends the ball my father had bought for me.

I remember it felt good to say the words *My father* because I hardly got to say them.

That was a long time ago. What Ma doesn't know is that Dad and I have been in touch by e-mail. He sent me a Facebook request a couple of years ago and since then we try to keep in touch. It's been about seven months since he messaged me, though.

'They say he is quite bad. So I thought I should let you know,' Ma says.

'I want to go and see him.'

Her mouth drops open. Shaking her head she says, 'I am only telling you. You don't need to go. He's very far away. In his village at his father's home.'

'We've been in touch by e-mail. I don't know why he didn't tell me he was-'

'You what?' Ma jumps to her feet and the cigarette she has been concealing in her clenched fist falls to the floor. We both ignore it. 'You've been in touch with him behind my back?'

'I didn't know I needed your permission to contact my father.' It was one of those moments when I knew I was saying something I knew I shouldn't say. But heck I have had a bad day, it couldn't get any worse.

'Bobo, are you questioning me after everything he's put us through?'

'All you've been through, Mum. I haven't been through anything with him. You kept him away from me, remember?'

'I did it for your sake. He was not a good role model for you.'

'Well, you didn't give him a chance to be a model of any kind in my life.'

She notices her cigarette on the floor and picks it up. Her hands are shaking. 'I know he's your father. But after all I have done I just thought you would tell me that you are in touch with him.'

'You make it sound as if he was a monster. As if he would harm me. If you feel that way why did you make me with him?' There is something that sets me off anytime we talk about my father. Now my blood is boiling. I feel it throbbing in my temples. 'Who asked you to do all you've done? You shouldn't have had me then.' I hear my voice in the distance, gruff with emotion. My anger must be showing because I can see fear in Ma's eyes. As I step up to her, she shrinks back.

I don't know why, but my whole body is shaking. I start to lose control. 'He's my father. You chose him not me. Now I contact him and you accuse me of betraying you!'

'He's never done anything for-'

'You chose him!' I scream, grabbing hold of her wrists. I bend down and bite the cigarette out of her clenched fist. I spit it aside, then stare into her face because I want her to understand me. To know how empty I sometimes feel, without a father. Ma tries to wriggle free, but my hands clasp her wrists as tight as handcuffs. 'Don't' you see? I didn't pick him!' Couldn't Ma see what she had done? She had created the situation and now she is making it my problem.

As I try to shake some sense into her, I see the humiliation in my old man's eyes and remember the pain I felt whenever he came to visit me and he was treated like a leper. I've never told anyone how it made me feel. I always act like I don't notice the way they treat him.

As the rage sears through me, I realise that I have held it in too long because now I can't stop it all tumbling out into Ma's horrified face. I hear Ma scream, only then do I see that I've pinned her against the cupboard. Before I can let go of her, Mwati rushes in.

'Ja, leave your mother!' He grabs hold of me but I free Ma and shake him off. 'Are you trying to kill your mother? Madam, are you okay?' I hear him ask as I run out of the house.

The last thing I hear Ma say in a rasp, 'I'm fine. I'm fine. But please go after Bobo. Make sure Bobo is okay.'

Chapter 3

Sula

I find Amai and her sister Amai Mukulu on the veranda furiously peddling their Bernina sewing machines. My mother, born six minutes after Amai Mukulu, is the smaller and calmer of the two. Looking at them, it's obvious who was in charge and who ate a bigger share of the food when they shared a home for nine months in my grandma's womb. And if you hang around the household they share now it soon becomes obvious who is still in charge. Bits of orange satin fabric are scattered everywhere. One of the chickens is scurrying about with orange thread attached to its claw. Both women look up and smile at me.

'Another wedding.' Amai Mukulu explains the orange mess. She winces, gets up, and stretches. 'I think it's enough for today,' she tells her sister.

'Sula, you're home later than usual,' Amai says. She starts to fold away the dress in her arms. She looks a bit distracted and doesn't seem to be waiting for my reply; I don't say anything.

'Why are your eyes red?' Amai Mukulu asks.

'I'm fine.' I start walking into the house. I have tried my best not to look like I've been crying but trust Amai Mukulu to pick up on it. To divert attention from myself I say, 'Both of you look tired. You should hire someone to help sew.'

'What? Bring in someone to spoil our business. We will sew ourselves right down to the last stitch and button,' Amai Mukulu says, picking a dress off Ma's lap and holding it out to me. 'Beautiful, isn't it?'

I nod and laugh before walking past them into the house. Then Amai says, 'Your sister is inside,' and I realise why she has been distracted. My stomach churns as I go in to find Joyce.

The first time I heard Bambo use foul language was when Amai and Amai Mukulu sat him down and told him Joyce was pregnant. 'The problem with Joyce,' Bambo yelled, 'is that she doesn't understand the proverb, everyone defecates, but smart people defecate at the bottom of the hill. Not Joyce. She defecates where she is standing and so all of us - including herself- end up in her smelly mess!'

Joyce is my elder sister. I have to say she can be wonderful most of the time. But I also have to admit that over the years Bambo's analogy about Joyce's rubbish being everywhere has become more and more apparent to me.

She is exactly four years older than me to the day. Slim, wide-eyed, pretty, and spoilt because for a time she was assumed an only child when Amai's efforts to conceive another proved fruitless for three years. Joyce was a hard act to follow. I was supposed to be the grand finale, particularly as Amai decided and announced to everyone that I was to be her last child. I turned out the sideshow. In comparison to Joyce I was quiet, fat, and words did not come out of my mouth sweet and soothing like honey or a love song the way they came out of Joyce's. It didn't take me long to realise I was different from Joyce. I saw the light go off in peoples' eyes when Joyce proudly announced that I was her little sister. They assumed that Joyce would have a sister like her so when I showed up they found it difficult to disguise their disappointment.

To be fair to Joyce, she tried to make me shine with her but I realised the more I stood beside her, the dimmer I felt. So I stopped trying to follow her or to be like her. Then Joyce turned fifteen and the problems started. She would go out and come home after curfew. Although she was very bright she stopped paying attention in school. She wasn't scared of anyone or anything. Bambo would punish her, lash her with his belt but the very next day she would go out and do exactly the same thing for which she had been lashed the day before. Eventually Bambo washed his hands of her. He said he didn't want to kill her and end up in jail, so he ignored her. That proved difficult because most times Joyce's troubles followed her all the way home. And although Bambo claimed to have disowned Joyce, when trouble came he stood up and rescued her. Just before her nineteenth birthday Joyce gave birth to Letti, a beautiful baby girl. After she had Letti, Joyce moved into a flat paid for by Letti's father. It has been two years since she moved out.

Joyce's exit was bittersweet; I missed her because she had a way of making me feel strong and safe. But then when she left I was pleased that I no longer had to live with the anticipation and anxiety in my stomach of what wrong Joyce was about to do. With Joyce it was not about whether she was going to mess up, but more about where, when, and how deep in her muck I would find myself.

When I get to the bedroom door I can't open it because something heavy has been put against it. 'Joyce, it's me,' I say through the door.

I hear Joyce shuffling around inside. Then she opens the door. When I walk in she's putting the chair she had up against the wall back in its place. She walks up to me, hugs me. Something is wrong. Joyce is fidgety and smells unlike her. She always has a whiff of perfume about her, but today I detect the acrid smell of sweat.

'What were you doing?'

'I was just trying on something. A dress I bought today,' Joyce says, playing with her braids. Before I can ask her why she barricaded the door she fishes a pair of flat red sandals from a plastic bag and hands it to me. 'Here, I bought these for you.'

Joyce is very generous to a point of recklessness. The money she gets from Letti's father slips through her fingers as if it were fine grain salt. But I have to say if it wasn't for her, my wardrobe would be full of the cotton shirts and summer dresses sewn by Amai and her twin sister. The sandals are very pretty. I thank Joyce, then take off my school shoes, and try the sandals on.

'So ....are you all ready for the dance?' Joyce asks.

I shake my head. 'Not going.'

'Why? What is the matter? Have you been crying?'

Because she asks I feel the tears well up in my eyes.

Joyce sits beside me. 'Do you have a partner for the dance?'

I shake my head again.

'Has anyone asked you?'

I hesitate. 'Ja asked me but I think he only did so because his friends dared him to.'

Joyce's eyes pop out 'Ja Maponya asked you? Then why aren't you going?'

'Because he wasn't serious.' I tell her how it happened. After I finish speaking, I notice Joyce's eyes are wide with excitement.

'Look,' she says, 'if he didn't want to take you he wouldn't have run after you. I think you should go.' Then she looks at her watch and says, 'Look, I'll be back. I have to dash off now. But I will help you get ready for the dance. I'll pick you up one of these days so we can go and buy a dress. Or fabric. And I will arrange to have your hair done. A Brazilian weave will look great on you.'

'But he wasn't serious. Plus I can't afford Brazilian hair.'

'He was serious; just leave the hair to me. Be positive. I have to go now.' Joyce picks up her bag and asks, 'Does anyone use that old suitcase up there?' She points at her old suitcase sitting on top of the wardrobe.

I tell her no one uses it and I ask her to bring Letti next time she comes.

'I will but I have to go now.' She suddenly looks anxious again. She tightens the red tie that is holding her locks together. She's talking to me about Ja as she sprays some of my deodorant in her armpits. 'He may come from a rich family but it doesn't mean he can't fall for you. Just be positive and act like he's not as great as he thinks he is.' I walk her out of the house and on to the verandah.

Amai and Amai Mukulu try to persuade Joyce to stay for dinner, to take some food for Letti, but Joyce tells them she has to rush.

'Where to?' Ami Mukulu asks. 'You have just come. Where are you rushing to? It's not like you work. And you said Letti is at home with Olipa.'

'I have business to do,' Joyce says. 'I will be back to help Sula decide on a dress and hairstyle for the dance.'

'The dance? I thought you weren't going?' Amai asks.

The two women look at me. So does my young sister Zafika who has just returned from school. Indeed, after all Amai said about not having another child when she was pregnant with me, Zafika arrived nine years later.

'I didn't say I was going nor did I say I wasn't,' I say.

'Sula said she won't go to the school dance because she doesn't like dancing,' Zafika says. 'But I think she won't go because no boy has asked her to the dance.' Zafika has a mouth that runs like a tap.

Her words stop Joyce in her tracks. She swings back and snaps at Zafika. 'She has a date. Ja Maponya has asked her to the dance and she is going to go.'

'Maponya?' Amai and Amai Mukulu chorus. They always say the same thing at the same time; sometimes they say and feel the same things even when they are miles apart.

'Yes. And why are you both so surprised? They have been lab partners for the two terms. They are friends.' Joyce finishes her sentence and rushes out the gate.

'Will you go?' Amai Mukulu asks.

I'm starting to feel irritated by the fact that the conversation around me is happening as if I'm not there. 'I am not going to the stupid dance!' I say. 'What is the big deal about a school dance? It's just boys and girls dressing up to eat for one hour and dance for two. What's the point?'

'It is a good experience,' says Amai Mukulu. 'You should go. In fact, I have a style for a beautiful dress that will make you look beautiful.'

'But Bambo won't allow her to go. He doesn't want her mixing with boys,' Zafika says. She looks around furtively to make sure Joyce is gone, then adds, 'He says he doesn't want her to end up like Joyce - baaaad.'

'Have you been listening to adult conversation?' Amai Mukulu asks. 'Get away from here!' She picks up her slipper and throws it at Zafika who ducks and disappears behind the wall giggling.

A few minutes later, as I take my shower, I listen to bits of Amai and Amai Mukulu's conversation. Their voices reach me through the window.

I hear Amai Mukulu say, 'Something is up with Joyce. She didn't seem herself. She was jumpy and in a great hurry. She didn't even want to eat today.'

'You also noticed?' Amai asks. Then with a sigh she adds, 'It only could mean one thing. Let's brace ourselves.'

Chapter 4

Ja

I'm an idiot. I keep saying it to myself just so I can feel better but it's not working. Mwati and I are in the Highlander, hitting 110 miles per hour on the dual carriageway to Sempa to see my old man.

If you had told me forty-eight hours ago that I would lay my hands on Ma, I would have laughed at the absurdity of the statement. Now I'm not laughing. In fact I'm freaked out at what I did. After I ran out of the house I wandered around for hours. Then when I got so tired and my leg began throbbing like a toothache, I limped back home and found Ma frantic.

She didn't say anything when I got home. I guess we were both trying to avoid another confrontation. The first words out of my mouth were an apology. I told her I had no idea what came over me but I would never touch her again. But, even though I was sorry about laying my hands on her, I had to go and see my old man. Ma did not argue. In fact, she was trying so hard to make peace that she agreed I could miss the last day of class so that I could go to Sempa for one night.

The sudden slowing motion of the car wakes me and I realise that I had dozed off. My music is still playing in my ears. I see my phone flashing. I'm not in the mood for texts from Mum, or Tiger, or Kenya, or whoever. But since I don't recognise the number curiosity gets the better of me. I TOLD YOU TO LET ME DO THE PROJECT. NOW YOU HAVE IT AND YOU HAVEN'T TURNED UP FOR SCHOOL. REMEMBER IT'S DUE MONDAY AND WE WERE SUPPOSED TO DISCUSS IT TODAY!!!!!!

Yikes, it's from Sula. It is all in capital letters so I guess she's shouting, even though I can't imagine her raising her voice. I had completely forgotten about the project. I pull off my earphones and dial Ma. She sounds surprised to hear from me. In a panicked voice I describe the folder and the usb to her and ask her to get them from my school bag and deliver them to Bellington where Sula lives.

'Where?' Ma sounds aghast. 'There's a girl in your class who lives in Bellington?'

'Ma, please just do it. She's my science partner and she always puts more into our projects than I do. I can't let her down.' I decide not to mention to Ma that the fight we had is the reason I forgot about the project. 'Please Ma. She's sent me a text message. I'll give you her number, so you can arrange to drop them off.' After I get off the phone I dial Sula's number. She doesn't pick up and I realise her phone is off because she is in class. And because she likes to follow school rules to the dotting of I and crossing of T, I know for sure that her phone will be off the whole day until she gets off school. I text her to say that Ma will deliver the usb and folder. I apologise for forgetting and tell her I'll do the whole project for the both of us next time, which is stupid because we are at the end of the year. I mention in the text which is now three texts long that my father is sick and I have to go and see him. And then out of guilt or perhaps stupidity, I add something to the effect that we need to discuss where we'll meet up to go to the dance. Only after I tap 'send' I realise that I can't turn back now because I've committed to taking her to the dance.

Seconds later my mobile rings; I recognise Sula's number.

'Hey aren't you in ?'

She cuts me short. 'I'm so tired of your stupid games! I told you to let me do the project! If I fail you'll see what I'll do to you!'

She's raving mad. I try to explain that I have an emergency and that my Mum will deliver the folder and the usb but she calls me a big mummy's baby and cuts the line.

I try to call her back, but I only get an automated voicemail. I switch the phone off, toss it aside. My leg is starting to hurt again, because I've been sitting in the same position for a while. The long walk I had yesterday after I stormed out has also taken its toll. Apart from the throbbing in my leg, I feel sore inside when I think of my fight with Ma, my sick father and now Sula. I am hurt because she didn't seem to care that my father is unwell and is just thinking about the project. But then again, I didn't care when I made her cry yesterday so I can't expect any sympathy from her. I pull on my headphones, close my eyes again and pray that sleep will come and take me away from my misery.

We arrive in Sempa at midday. It has just stopped raining heavily, the road is all muddy and water gushes along the road sides. The directions we have are to get to the main transmitter station and ask anyone there for the postmaster's house. We find the transmitter after stopping a few places to ask, it is a high tower of metal poles and wires standing behind a small white block in need of space fenced in by a high wire mesh fence.

A group of young boys are walking past, they pause and then walk over to the jeep. Mwati asks for the postmaster's house and the group leader (I can tell he's the leader from the way he struts over to us, leading the pack, with a football lodged in the triangle of his elbow) says, 'That is my house. I'll show you where it is.' Before Mwati can say anything the boy opens the car door and climbs in to the front seat.

'I asked you to show us where the house is not to get in-' Mwati starts to say but I intervene, for I know the boy is only trying to show off to his friends.

'It's okay, let him drive with us.'

Mwati eyes the boy's dusty knees and his muddy football before starting the car.

As we pull away the boy throws his ball out to his friends and asks them to keep it clean.

'You had better know where we are going,' Mwati says.

'I do,' the boy replies with a wide smile.

I like the way the boy is not intimidated by Mwati. He directs us off the main road and down a wide gravel road. A few houses are scattered alongside the road. We turn off again and the boy asks Mwati to park because if we go any further the jeep will get stuck in the mud.

'Just show me where to go. I am the driver. I will decide whether we'll get stuck or not.' Mwati sounds testy, obviously irritated by the boy.

'Master, everyday, cars get stuck there by that turning in front,' the boy insists. He explains that Mwati can't park the car nearer the turn because the car would block the road. 'It is best to leave it here where it will not get stuck and it's not blocking other cars.' He opens the door and jumps out. 'Follow me.'

We leave the Highlander and follow him. He is wearing oversize trainers which he has attached to his feet by tying the black laces around his ankles. He offers to carry my bag but I tell him it's okay. We manoeuvre our way across big puddles of water by balancing on stones laid out for pedestrians to step on. After the swamp we follow the boy along a footpath. We walk past a few mud brick houses, the women and children around the houses call out greetings to the boy. He returns their greetings and salutes them. He is obviously pleased by the attention we are drawing to ourselves and to him. The people stop and stare, curious to know who Mwati and I are.

Mwati keeps asking the boy if the car is safe. 'Master it's safe where we leave it. If we left it in town near the bus stop, it would not be safe,' the boy speaks with the confidence of a streetwise youth.

I ask him what his name is.

'Eric.'

'I am Ja.'

The boy stops abruptly and swings around to face me. I almost knock him over because I didn't expect him to stop. He smiles at me showing his big white teeth. And before I can ask him what he's smiling about, he steps forward and wraps his arms around my waist. I'm not sure what to do, I'm conscious of the people watching and embarrassed at the boy's display of affection. Not sure what to do I get hold of his arms and try to gently unwind them from around my body. Eric steps back and says, 'You're my brother!'

Mwati and I stare at him, then at each other.

'Who are you?' Mwati asks, almost snickering.

'I am Eric. Son of Daniel Kalulu, the grandson of the Postmaster General senior Kalulu. Ja,' Eric points at me and turns to Mwati, 'is my brother. My father told me I have a big brother called Ja.'

I am too shocked to speak. I don't want Mwati to interrogate Eric any longer as I know he is telling the truth. So I say to Mwati, 'Yes this is my half brother.'

We walk the rest of the way in silence. Eric with a big smile on his face holds my hand tightly and I am grateful for it because I suddenly feel weak in the knees.

We mount steep concrete steps to a big old house. I have been here once before many, many years ago when my grandfather was alive. On the verandah, we find a tall dark woman with big eyes whom Eric introduces as his mother. He also introduces me to his two younger sisters who are not a great surprise because Eric has filled me in. His mother seems to know who I am. She says her name is Auntie Jean and greets us warmly. Then she offers us two old springy chairs while she hurries around, I imagine, making impromptu arrangements to accommodate us.

Mwati and I sit on the verandah, silent again, watching the activity below us. Cars and buses move in what seems like slow motion along a winding road below us. We see rooftops of varying shapes and sizes amongst lush green treetops. It is the rainy season and grass and trees are all a deep green. Eric has disappeared, probably ran back to play football. His little sister steps onto the verandah and sets a tray of bottled water and two glasses on a table between Mwati and me. She pours the water and hands us the glasses with a small curtsy. I notice that her dress, although un-hemmed, is a bit short for her. I suddenly feel sad. I decide that I will buy gifts for everyone before I leave with '*the just in case*' money Ma gave me. I try to make conversation with the young girl but I can see she is rather shy, so I let her escape as soon as she has poured the water into the glasses.

There is movement down the path and I see a young man walk up the path and jog up the stairs. He looks to be a few years older than me, perhaps in his early twenties. He shakes my hand, then Mwati's hand, and introduces himself as George. He calls out for a chair and the young girl emerges with a stool on which George perches. He says Auntie Jean called him and he happened to be close by. Conversation seems to come naturally to him, he starts to talk about the heavy rain and how the new mine is changing the town.

'Not all change is good,' George says when Mwati says that the new mines will bring about development. 'They are cutting down the trees, moving people from their homes, and using up large supplies of water such that the taps for the locals are running dry.'

George explains how the mines are having a negative impact on the community. He talks non-stop. I know what my Papa would say to him, something he always said to me when I was growing up: 'No matter how much knowledge you have, and how strong your views, always take the time to listen to what other people have to say. You might learn something new.'

Although he talks a lot, I take a liking to George. He seems honest about his views and passionate about Sempa. He tells us he works as a Project Officer for Live and Grow, an NGO that tries to teach communities how to sustain themselves. I ask him if he thinks that African communities were unable to sustain themselves before the western NGOs came to town.

George jumps up and high fives my hand against his. 'You've hit the nail on the head, my brother,' he says. 'I work for these people and yes I know that we have to start preserving our resources. But I tell them that our societies have lived in harmony with their environment for as long as they have been in existence. That our communities have had their own methods of preserving and sustaining their environment. I want them to understand that they are not teaching us anything new.'

George eventually has to leave for a meeting he has at 2 p.m. He says he'll be back for me later in the afternoon so he can take me to the hospital and show me where he works. I am relieved to have met him. As I watch him walk away I can't wait for him to come back. He has made me feel comfortable whereas everything and everyone around me since I arrived in Sempa has made me feel awkward and out of place. In Sempa I feel as if I am a new piece of furniture in an old house.

Auntie Jean joins us on the verandah and announces lunch will be ready soon. She asks if I'm okay going to the hospital with George; I assure her I'll be fine with him. She explains that Eric has gone to the guest house down the road to use the Internet café, to print something for his homework. He's at a Christian boarding school and has only come home for the weekend. She explains that the computer in the house has not been working for a while. I know she's just talking to fill the time, but I think of the two computers sitting unused in the spare room at home. I decide that I will send the newer one to Eric and his sisters. Auntie Jean leaves Mwati and me to eat lunch alone.

After we are through Mwati tells Auntie Jean that he will be driving back and will come for me the following morning. Auntie Jean looks a bit worried.

'I'll be fine. George says he'll show me around,' I say. But then she asks. 'Does your mother know that he is leaving you here?'

Mwati assures Auntie Jean that that was the arrangement.

Auntie Jean nods, but I can see in her face that she is unsure about the arrangement. I know what is making Auntie Jean apprehensive. Ma has that effect on people. Even those who have never met her.

Chapter 5

Sula

I can't believe that I called Ja a mummy's boy and that I hung up on him. I switched on my phone during my break time and saw missed calls from Ja, but I was too scared to return them. I spent my day wondering what I would do if his mother didn't bring the folder. My fear is that a low mark in the project work will mean less chance of me getting an A+ in Chemistry. Then just as the bell rung for the end of the day my phone rang. The ringtone set my heart beating like a drum in my ears. I guessed who it was because I didn't recognise the number. She introduced herself as Hannah Maponya.

I kept quiet, unsure of how to greet her. She repeated her introduction, I guess from my silence she thought I hadn't heard the first time. She said her son Ja was off sick and he had asked her to deliver a yellow science folder and a usb. I wondered why she lied about Ja being sick. She obviously didn't know he had told me that he was going to visit his sick father.

When I finally engaged my brain and mouth, I asked Hannah Maponya if she could drop the folder at the school reception. I wanted to wait for her at the school because I didn't want her to come to Bellington but she said she was very busy at work and could not come right away. She sounded exasperated as she listed the things she had to do. She spoke as if I was the one who was causing her to drive across town. In my head I said, *Madam, it's your son that has caused you the inconvenience.* However, into the receiver I said, 'Sorry madam for the inconvenience, but can you please drop it at the reception tomorrow morning? The school reception stays open till noon on Saturday and I will pick it up.'

After a very difficult conversation - I couldn't hear what she was saying above the loud beating of my heart and she was irritated with having to repeat herself she insisted that on Ja's instructions she would get the folder to me today Friday. When I told her, because I had no option, that I lived in Bellington she said, 'I know,' and then she asked me how long I had been at St. Mathews and who I lived with in Bellington. At that point I wondered how Ja knew where I lived but of course I didn't say anything. I gave her directions and hung up. So that is how I ended up in a situation where Ja's mother is coming to my house. If Joyce knew about this she would kill me.

The first thing I tell Amai when I get home is that Ja's mother is coming by.

'Why did you let Ja take the folder in the first place?' Amai asks. She's placed a damp handkerchief over a freshly sewn skirt and is ironing it with a heavy metal iron that heats up by putting hot coal inside. The two sisters think a charcoal iron works much better than an electric one.

'He said I always do the work so he would do it this time.'

'Do you have the time to do it?'

'What folder?' Amai Mukulu steps out of the house.

'Ja's mother is coming to bring a folder,' I say.

Amai fills her sister in and when she finishes Amai Mukulu turns to me and asks, 'Does she know that her son has asked you to the dance?'

'He hasn't invited me.' They both look at me funny so I add, 'I mean he asked but he was joking.' With that I walk into the house. But Amai Mukulu isn't about to let me off easily. She follows me into the bedroom and closes the door.

'Sweetie, what is happening?'

Suddenly I feel like crying.

'Tell me, do you want to go to the dance or not?'

I tell her I'm not sure. I tell her I think Ja only asked me because his friends challenged him. I confess that I would love to go with him but I don't want to be made a fool of. Amai Mukulu wants to know why I think Ja wouldn't be serious about taking me to the dance. And I explain that he is the most popular boy in the school, he's mother is a VIP, he's great at sports and music and he's very clever. To make me feel better Amai Mukulu says, 'And you are very, very clever, you have a beautiful voice which is a great talent, and you are very special. And by the way, in God's eyes we are all VIPs!'

I smile at her words but I think we both understand why I am feeling awkward. I go in and take my shower as I have a choir practice later in the evening. While dressing up, I hear Amai and Amai Mukulu talking. I know she is filling Amai in with every word I said in spite of the fact that she promised not to share.

Ja's ma calls for directions and I give them to her: *Turn off the main Road at Good Times Bottle store, it is painted bright pink. Then take the 3rd left at the big car park station surrounded by an unpainted wall with coiled barbed wire running along the top. I don't add that that is the car park where Bambo parks the company car he drives so that it doesn't get stolen. Drive down to the T junction and turn right, you'll see an old red truck and a big yellow MTN sign ahead of you. The house is the 4th after the truck and the sign. It's a high wall with a black gate. House number fourteen.*

She lets me finish giving her the directions, then she sighs and says, 'I can't remember all that. I'll call you when I get to the bottle store.' She calls thrice. The second time I mistakenly ask her to turn left instead of right at the T junction. So I lose her completely. Amai Mukulu, who is standing by me through the conversations, takes the phone from me and directs Ja's Ma to the house. By the end of the conversation Amai Mukulu is seething. She heaves, 'No wonder the country is in shambles, she heads the country's water company and yet she can't even follow simple directions, hai!'

Amai Mukulu stops me from waiting at the gate. She says, 'Miss-Speak-English-Through-The-Nose can very well get out of her car, walk to the door, and knock.'

When Miss-Speak-English-Through-The-Nose arrives she honks at the gate and before Amai Mukulu can stop me I rush out to the car. I greet her politely and apologise for getting her lost. She stares at me in a way that makes me feel very small; a nuisance. I am ready to go to choir practice and I have worn my jeans and a blue shirt which Joyce gave me. I have tied my hair back with a piece of navy and mustard batik print cloth left over from one of Amai's customers' fabric. Yet I am irritated that I made an effort for this woman who stares down at me from the window of her four by four.

The sun has set but she still has her sunglasses perched on her head like a hair band. Her hair is obviously a weave, it's too brown, too silky to be her natural hair.

'So how long have you been at St. Mathews?' That is her first question.

I'm sure she's already asked me on the phone but again I tell her that it is my second year and final year of 'A' Level.

'And you did your Grade 12 at Bellington High?'

I nod. She remembers the details of our earlier conversation. I can see that she's trying to add things up; Bellington High a low funded, non-fee paying government school for girls to St Mathew's the most expensive private school in the country does not add up. To end the conversation and even though she hasn't handed it over, I say, 'Thank you so much for bringing the folder and the usb.'

She reaches over to get the folder but to my horror, Amai Mukulu walks out of the gate and towards the car.

'Hello, so you finally found us?' Amai Mukulu asks.

'Finally. It's not easy to find, no road signs or anything.' Ja's mother waves her hands about to signal the absence of road names. Then she looks at the usb and asks, 'Did you write these names?'

I shake my head. 'Ja labelled it because he has more than one usb of the same colour,' I explain.

'Well, that's how we live in these parts.' Amai Mukulu is back to the conversation of Bellington. 'We have no road signs, no books in schools, no medicines in our local clinic and no water.'

I see the anger in Ja's mother's face so I quickly say, 'I am going for choir practice now, madam. May I please take the folder?'

'All these problems will be solved soon,' Ja's mother says, handing me the folder and the usb. 'We're working to improve all social services.'

To deter a response from Amai Mukulu I hand her the folder and ask her to put it in the house for me. She takes it but doesn't walk away. She stands by the car, folder in hand, waiting for me to go. I can't leave the two of them together, so I take the folder back and say that I'll take it in myself. But Amai Mukulu holds on to it. 'I will take it in. You head off for choir practice.' Turning back to Ja's mother she says, 'Well, so we're told before the elections. Things will change but once they have our votes we don't see any change.'

Ja's mother laughs. A laugh that suggests what Amai Mukulu has just said is absurd. She responds, 'Change takes time. I can assure you the signs are there that things are getting better.'

Just when I think things can't get any worse Bambo arrives in his uniform, navy shirt, navy trousers and navy and grey striped tie. As usual, a newspaper is tucked under his arm and he's carrying the black holdall he takes with him whenever he goes out of town. The car has blocked our gateway so to walk in Bambo has to squeeze right past the car window.

'Good evening,' he says to Ja's mother, nods at Amai Mukulu, turns to me, then asks, 'Are you not late for choir practice?'

'I'm going now. Madam here is my science partner's mother and she just brought my science project.' A question registers on Bambo's face so I explain further. 'We have a science project to do. It's due on Monday and my partner is sick so his mother has brought the folder.'

'Haven't you left it late? If it's due on Monday why is it not done yet?' Bambo asks and I wish I hadn't explained.

'Sula has done her bit. It's the partner who is unable to do his part so that is why Sula has - '

Ja's mother does not allow Amai Mukulu to finish. 'My son has a problem. He has had to travel. It's not his fault.'

'I am saying Sula is doing it because your son is unable to. I did not say it was your son's fault. Just as I am not saying it's Sula's fault.'

'This is a small matter.' Ja's mother's tone is starting to match Amai Mukulu's. 'I can ask the school to extend the deadline so my son does his bit.'

'Why should Sula get an extension because of your son?' Amai Mukulu asks.

Bambo looks uneasy. The two women are starting to raise their voices. Before Ja's mother can match Amai Mukulu's tone he asks, 'Sula, can you get it done by Monday?' I nod. He addresses Amai Mukulu, 'Then let her do it.' He looks at his watch. 'You'll be late for choir practice. Next time make sure the work is done on time. Have a good evening, madam,' he says to Ja's mother and disappears inside the gate.

I say goodbye and thank you to Ja's mother. I start to walk away, wishing I were somewhere else. If only I had stood my ground with Ja and taken the folder home in the first place. As I walk away I think I hear Amai Mukulu say the word dance. Then I stop listening because my head is spinning, disappointment burns inside me. I wish I hadn't entertained the idea of Ja as my partner at the dance. Because I know after Amai Mukulu has finished with Hannah Maponya there is no way she will allow her son to be my partner at the dance.

Chapter 6

Ja

We drive through the centre of Sempa and it's like watching a film about an ancient town. George gives a running commentary, pointing out when buildings were built and their significance to the town. We drive along a straight road past a few dusty buildings, a grocery store, a fast-food takeaway, a filling station, a freshly painted bank and Shoprite supermarket.

'The so-called signs of development,' George, who is at the wheel of his company's bright yellow Hilux, says as we turn onto a newly tarred road with clear white markings. 'Everyone made a lot of noise about this road. It will bring jobs, development, etc. It's been here a year, what has it brought? The people here do not have the means to use this road, they have nowhere to go. So they watch the big cars and trucks speed past.'

'Was it built for access?'

'The mines say they built it for the people but the people here don't need a road, they need jobs before they can even start to think of using the road. Very few locals were employed to build this road and the irony is that it is used mainly by the mines. They built it for themselves.'

I think to myself that a road at least makes the town accessible so that has to be a good thing but I keep quiet as George lives in the place so he should know. I am amazed at how a young modern guy like George can live in a deadbeat place like Sempa.

George slows down and turns into a gate. 'This is the new hospital. Built by the Chinese.'

My heart starts to beat at the thought of seeing my old man in person after eight years. George senses my anxiety. Before we step out of the car, he holds me on the upper arm and, looking straight into my eyes, says, 'He's not doing very well.'

I nod and start to get out of the car. I try to walk briskly behind George to hide that my stomach is churning and my heart pounding. I follow George past the reception where a nurse greets him cheerily. We pass through swing doors and down a narrow corridor with closed numbered doors running along it. The smell of the place reminds me of when I last saw Nana my grandmother just before she passed away. She was lying in a hospital bed. Her mouth in a smile but her eyes kept staring at nothing. I have hated hospitals since then.

We get to a bench in the corridor and George stops to greet the old, bald man sitting on it, then turns to me: 'This is your Dad's uncle. So he's your grandfather.' The old man jumps to his feet and clasps both my hands in his. He has on a thick red jumper over his white shirt and a red tie. His hands are rough and wrinkled but have a strong grip. I am forced to sit beside him because he sits down with his hand still gripping mine. George quickly excuses himself and shunts off to sit on a bench a few doors ahead. The old man bends his head and starts to cry. I don't know what to do. I feel a lump growing in my throat but I manage to hold it down. The old man pulls out a white ironed handkerchief, shakes it open and wipes his face.

'I am sad,' he whispers. 'Because you have reminded me of my younger brother, your grandfather.'

I nod.

'He was a good hard working man, you know.'

I nod again.

He asks me after a while, 'When did you last see him? Your father?'

'Eight years ago,' I answer.

The old man shakes his head. 'He is different now.' He sounds quite distraught. 'He is very sick.'

I feel an urge to shut my eyes. Instead I exhale, then ask, 'What is wrong with him?'

The old man jabs at his ribs. 'His kidneys are gone.'

'Can't anything be done?'

'Some new doctors are coming next week. They'll assess and decide. But don't worry, God will prevail. I can see you are a strong young man. You go inside and see him.' He beckons to George and asks him to lead me in.

My old man is lying on his side facing the door. The bed is resting alongside the white wall. He lifts his head as we walk in, peers expectantly. He smiles, and although I see that his skin is blacker and his hair greyer, his smile is the same. Sad. I wonder if he naturally has a sad smile or whether I am the one who conjures up a sadness in him that carries through his smile because I have never seen him smile any other way.

'You have come,' he says through cracked lips. As if reading my mind, he reaches across to the side table and dips his finger into a small tub of Vaseline and balms his lips. 'I am so happy you have come.'

I notice his fingernails are black. I help him up as he struggles to pull himself up. The bonness of his arm startles me. So I let go of him as soon as he rests his back against the metal bed frame.

He greets George, then apologises for the fact that he has not washed his face and brushed his teeth. 'We have no water today,' he says. His words hit me in the stomach. I look at George who gives me an *I-told-you-things-were-bad* shrug.

'Did you travel well?'

I nod but my eyes are on two empty jerrycans.

'Can't we go and get you some water?'

'Don't worry. Your Auntie Jean will bring more water later. I had enough for today but a man was very sick in the other room so the nurse asked if she could use some of my water to clean him.' He explains then again asks, 'Did you travel well?'

George excuses himself again. I sit down and start to tell him about my trip. I tell him how we got lost and how we stumbled across Eric who showed us the way. My old man sits back and listens with a smile. I notice the sadness lift from his smile, and he looks peaceful. Sometimes he closes his eyes but I can tell he is listening because every so often he asks me a question.

The door opens. I think it's George, and I look up, but only to see the old man shuffle in. I stand up to offer him my chair. But he declines and says he will stand instead, since he won't be staying long.

'So have you been talking to your son?' he asks my father who nods.

'Danny, talk to your boy here. Explain yourself. Most of us fathers show our sons the way through our actions. We set an example by living a life that sets a path they can follow.' The old man points at me. 'Now unless you want this young man to lead a life of sowing children everywhere and not bringing them up properly. I can only suggest that you use this time, these few minutes that you have, this blessing you have that God has made this boy come here, to tell him what you have failed to show him.'

At this point I start to feel anger towards the old man, it prickles in my ears. Can't he cut my old man some slack? Now is not the time to put him down.

'I don't enjoy standing here and saying this but we have to face the truth.' The old man turns to me. 'You are a young man growing up, you may also make mistakes in your life so what I am trying to do, as a useless old man, is to show you that our actions, the things we do on this earth, have consequences.' He moves forward and rests his hand on the bed to support himself. 'Your father had all the opportunities in the world. He went to the best schools, that is how he met your mother. He should not be lying here, in a village hospital with no water. He should be working abroad. But he chose his actions. He chose not to take the opportunities he had. And here are the consequences.'

My father is breathing heavily, I see his fists are clenched. 'Why Malume? Why talk like this in front of my son?' he says.

'So he doesn't make the same mistake.'

'I will talk to my son. It is my duty not yours.'

The old man sneers and says, 'Okay it is not my duty. I will leave you to do your duty. Talk to your son.' With that he turns away and shuffles out.

My father and I sit quietly for a while. Then he says, 'That old man is a troublemaker. Always has been, always will be.'

We remain quiet, until he coughs and says, 'I am sorry Ja. If I had another chance, I would do things differently. I messed up at an early age. I should have rectified everything when you were born but I didn't. I continued to fool around, didn't take my studies seriously. I thought my old man would always be there to bail me out. When he died I just couldn't cope. Don't be like me.'

Suddenly I have to leave the room. I pick up a jerrycan. 'Let me get you some water,' I offer.

He calls after me to stop me. But I don't turn back. I stumble out the room and down the corridor.

I start heading for the taps I had seen outside the hospital building. There is a queue at the two taps. I feel my heart sink as I observe people squabbling and jostling one another, just to fill their containers with water. Anyway, before I can get to the queue the nurse who had greeted George earlier at the reception catches up with me and tells me she already has someone in the queue filling up water for my father. She takes the empty can from my hand and leads me back to the reception.

On our way back, she asks if I'm okay. I tell her I'm fine. I just find a quiet corner outside where I can call my mother. She leaves me alone. When Ma picks up the phone, I hear myself yell at her. I ask her what she does at work all day while hospitals in the country are running without water. I tell her there are no young people in Sempa because there are no jobs. I tell her the road running through Sempa is a white elephant's project. To end my conversation, I vow to return to Sempa, after my exams. I make sure she heard that I will be donating one of my kidneys to help save my father. Then I cut the line.

Without thinking, I smash my phone to the ground as hard as I can.

Chapter 7

Sula

I wake up in the middle of the night to the voices of Amai and Amai Mukulu floating outside on the verandah. My heart starts beating. I get up, open the door quietly, and creep along the dark corridor to the living room where Amai Mukulu is on her mobile phone. The words tumble out of her mouth fast and jumbled; then she screams.

'If you touch that girl there will be hell to pay!'

Bambo stumbles into the living room pulling on his pyjama top. He squints as the light hits his face. 'What's happening?' he asks.

Amai is sitting on the centre table hugging herself and crying.

'He's killing her!' screams Amai Mukulu.

Bambo tries to wrestle the phone from her but she won't let go. She keeps screaming into the phone to whoever is on the other end. 'Bring her here! Bring her home if you don't want her!' Eventually Bambo manages to grab the phone but from the way he throws his arms up in the air and shakes his head I can tell that whoever is on the other end has hung up.

'What is happening here?!'Bambo shouts. 'What is happening in my house that I can't sleep?' He points at Amai. 'So you are making phone calls about my daughter who is in danger without waking me up? Is she not my daughter? Where is she? I'm going to get her.' Papa rushes back into his room.

'How can you go for her when you don't know where she is?' Amai stands up. She bounces up and down from one foot onto the other as if the ground is burning her feet. She whimpers but no one can hear what she is saying.

'He said he is on his way here,' says Amai Mukulu. She rushes into her room and dashes out almost immediately, pulling a jumper over her nightdress. She unlocks the door, and we all run outside.

We see headlights approaching and hear tyres crunching on gravel. The car is moving fast. The smell of burning rubber scorches the air. The car screeches to a halt. We all race towards the gate to open it. As Amai Mukulu hastily unlocks the padlock, we can hear Joyce screaming. We can hear the sound of flesh being pounded. Amai drops to her knees at the sound. I start shivering violently. The sound of Joyce screaming out in pain makes me cry out.

Bambo rushes out of the house clutching the iron bar we use to bar the door in his hand. He stamps out, his eyes wide open, and bangs the bar on the gate. We all jump back. Amai tries to hold him back, she tries to grab hold of the iron rod, but Bambo holds on to it, like a vice-grip.

The gates open; we tumble out, Amai Mukulu, Bambo with Amai trying to hold him back, myself and Zafika who is howling at the top of her voice. Our elderly neighbour Amake Miriam and her grandson Pastor Jose have come to see what the commotion is about. Pastor Jose holds Bambo back. Another male neighbour arrives and they manage to scramble Bambo back inside the gate; they obstruct him so he cannot get out. Amai Mukulu rushes up to Letti's daddy Mo and crashes into him with the full weight of her body; he falls backwards onto the bonnet of his car. He picks himself up instantly. He is very tall and slim but he has big hands which he uses to clasp Amai Mukulu's hands together so that she cannot hit him.

'Mum,' he says to Amai Mukulu, 'you are like a mother to me. I can't fight with you. I am here for my money. Give me my money and I will go.'

'I don't have your money,' shrieks Joyce. I am holding her back so she is shrieking into my ear. From the other side of the gate Bambo is shouting out what he will do to Mo while Amai and Pastor Jose are trying to calm him down.

As the screaming and scuffling goes on, a car draws up and two uniformed police officers, one male and one female, jump out.

'Arrest her!' Mo points at Joyce. 'She's stolen my money!'

Amake Miriam jumps in front of us and steers us towards the gate so the police cannot get to Joyce.

'What sort of policemen are you?' Amai asks. 'This child has been beaten up by this man but you want to arrest her and not him?' She points at Mo. 'How much has he bribed you?'

'There are two cases here. We are here about a domestic matter, madam,' says the policeman. 'This man has informed us that this is his wife. Has he not paid dowry?'

'Dowry does not mean he can kill her?' Amai Mukulu shouts. 'You should arrest him for beating her.'

'She has not filed a case against her husband,' says the policewoman who has bright red lipstick on her lips, I can see it in the moonlight. 'When she reports the case, we will arrest him. Now we are here because he has reported a theft and his wife is the main suspect.'

The policeman asks Mo to stand aside and the policewoman asks Amake Miriam to bring Joyce out. The crowd around us has grown; they have come to witness yet another episode in the Temani family drama starring Joyce Temani.

'If you don't want my daughter you bring her back. Don't kill her,' Amai says.

The policeman flashes his torch in Joyce's face and the crowd lets out a gasp. The left side of her face is the size of an orange and a trail of blood runs from her nostril to her mouth. Her bottom lip is bloody and swollen.

'I don't want this bitch. I want my money!' Mo hisses. He is panting. 'This bitch has stolen my four thousand dollars.'

In response Joyce spits a blob of bloody saliva into Mo's face. He lunges at her and everyone dives in to separate them.

Bambo agrees to surrender his iron rod and the police officers allow him out of the gate.

'Joyce,' Bambo asks, his voice low but shaking with anger. 'I will ask you only once. Have you taken this man's money?'

Joyce shakes her head at Bambo. Then Pastor Jose says in the American accent he acquired having spent two years in Colorado studying theology, 'Joyce, are you saying upon the name of God, our maker, our saviour, our lord, that you did not have this man's money?'

'Pastor, in God's name. I did not take his money,' Joyce says.

'You did Joyce. And you won't get away with it,' Mo snarls. 'If you don't bring it back, I'll kill you.'

Before Joyce can respond to Mo, Bambo points at the two police officers and Mo. 'You, you and you I give you permission to go inside my house and look for the money,' he says. 'Pray, and I repeat pray, you find it. Because if you don't I will report you for trespassing on my property.' He stands aside and opens the gate wide. Mo and the police officers hesitate.

The policeman says, 'Sir, we have to investigate all reports of theft. That is all we are doing.'

'And the abuse?' Amai Mukulu asks.

'As I explained earlier, your daughter can file assault charges and we will investigate. But the two incidents are different,' the policewoman says. From the way she sighs and keeps looking at the screen of her mobile phone it's obvious she wants to leave.

'So today I am a villain?' Mo shakes his head; he must have also read madam police woman's body language. 'I have given this girl everything, accommodation, put expensive clothes on her back and look at how she repays me.'

'But sir, the child is yours,' says the policeman. 'This woman is your wife and she says she did not take your money. We have no warrant to search the house so there is nothing we can do today. We are leaving now.'

Mo says he will be back for his money and to take Letti away, then he jumps into his car and drives off. Joyce jeers after him. The police leave, shortly after commenting on how surprised they are at Joyce's resilience. They cannot imagine how she is still standing and being defiant after all the blows Mo rained down on her. When they also drive off Bambo holds the gate open. We file past him, Amai, Amai Mukulu, Zafika, myself.

But when Joyce who is last in line tries to enter, Bambo holds his hand up and says, 'You are not welcome here. Go and shit somewhere else.' Then he closes the gate and clamps the heavy padlock shut.

****

I lie in wait for Zafika to start snoring. Meanwhile, I can hear my parents and Amai Mukulu settling back into their rooms, although I doubt any one of us apart from Zafika will be doing any sleeping tonight. My heart is still beating after all the fracas. I am not worried about Joyce being outside because I know Amake Miriam will take her in for the night. When the house becomes still I get up and place a chair up against the door handle such that it cannot open if someone tried to walk in from the outside. Then I climb onto the dressing table and lever Joyce's blue suitcase off the wardrobe. I am not sure what I am going to find but I can hear my heart thumping in my ears.

Gently, I lift the neatly packed clothes from the case and place them on the bed. It is just like Joyce to pack clothes she has disregarded neatly. She is compulsively tidy, folds everything all the time. Sharing a room with her was a nightmare. Every time I left something in one place I would return to find it stacked away neatly in another.

I feel around using the beam from the outside light to search as I don't want to switch on the light and wake Zafika. In the middle of the case I feel a hard bundle and I pull it out. It is a baby's blanket wrapped around a bag. My heart thumping harder, I open the canvas back to the light and peer inside. My heart stops for a moment. In the bag are thick wads of money held together by rubber bands. My hands start shaking. I take out a bundle: one hundred US dollar notes!

I drop the money back in the bag and start to fold it back into the towel, then I change my mind. I try to think straight. To sort out the questions spinning in my head. Should I tell Amai? Or Bambo, or the Police? Should I pretend not to know? Should I throw the money away before the police come back with a search warrant? All my questions have answers that scare me. All the answers spell serious trouble for Joyce. Because somehow I suspect that like me, Bambo knows that even though Joyce swore upon God that she didn't take the money, she did.

I get up early the next morning, have a quick bath and leave the house. I take a pair of jeans for Joyce and a fresh shirt. Like I guessed, I find her at Amake Miriam's house. Wrapped in a chitenge cloth, she is sitting outside on an upturned metal bucket and sipping tea through her bruised lip. Even with a purple eye she looks pretty. She also looks as if she has had more sleep than I have had. I know for a fact that Bambo, Amai and Amai Mukulu have not slept, but here is Joyce as bright as sunshine.

'Hi.' She gets up and hugs me. She smells of soap. Her makeup bag and sandals have been washed and they are drying on an old newspaper.

'I have brought you some clothes.' I hand the plastic bag to Joyce and at her beckoning, I follow her into Amake Miriam's house.

Amake Miriam has been our neighbour since forever and because of it she knows all the families in the neighbourhood and all their personal business. She is the one who first realised that Joyce was pregnant and whispered her suspicions to Amai Mukulu. And when Bambo kicked his wife and her twin sister out of his house one day many years ago, it was Amake Miriam who came and knelt before him and begged him to take them back into his house. If houses were human you would say our house and Amake Miriam's house were like identical twins. The layout is the same, the floor tiles are the same as they were laid by the same contractor and the curtains in the living room are the same as ours because Amai Mukulu sewed both sets of curtains from a big bale of fabric she and Amake Miriam bought jointly in Dubai.

We get to a bedroom and Joyce drops her chitenge and wriggles into the jeans I've brought for her. 'These jeans are a bit tight?' She wriggles exaggeratedly to make me laugh but I don't. So she puts on the white shirt and a serious face, then she sits beside me.

'Sula, sorry about yesterday. You know Mo is a mad man. I don't know what makes him think I took his money.'

'Liar!' I jump up, open my laptop bag, and yank out the green bag. 'So you didn't take it?' I shove the bag in her surprised face.

Joyce stands up and puts on her innocent face. Her head bowed, she says, 'That man owes me a lot. I have given him Letti but he will never marry me. How am I?'A knock at the door interrupts her. It opens and we both reach for the green bag which falls to the floor and Joyce manages to kick it under the bed just before Amai Miriam's head pops round the door.

'Is everything okay?' She's looking at me but Joyce answers.

'We're fine, auntie.'

'Sula?' I nod at Amake Miriam; she hands Joyce the makeup bag and the sandals. 'Joyce, when you finish dressing I want to talk to you both.'

I hiss at Joyce as soon as Amake Miriam closes the door. 'Last night you swore by God's name that you didn't have his money. You swore to Bambo and the Pastor that you hadn't taken the money.'

'Well, I didn't steal it. I took it. He owes me.' Joyce retrieves the bag from under the bed and puts in a plastic bag with her clothes from the previous night. 'Look. Sorry I lied last night but what was I supposed to do? If you were me would you say, *yes Bambo I took the money and it's in Sula's bedroom.'*

'I wouldn't lie when Bambo is trying to protect me. I wouldn't lie to a Pastor.'

'Mo is a crook. That is why he has so much money. It isn't rightfully his either.'

'It isn't yours, Joyce!'

Joyce sighs. 'Sula pleeeeez, don't give me a hard time.' She takes my hands in hers and faces me. 'We're sisters. Let's not fight. I promise not to lie again. But try and understand. I want to leave Mo but that means I have to find a way to fend for myself.' She leans in and whispers, 'Don't tell anyone that I have the money. I need it to make clean break from Mo and to start my life again. I have a plan. But I need money.'

'Go back to college. Stealing is not...'

'Look at me, Sula. Unlike you, I'm not going to get a scholarship to study for a degree and get a good job because I am not clever like you and I have Letti to look after.' Joyce gets up and starts applying her makeup in the mirror.

As she covers her bruises with foundation, a text message beeps through on my phone. I look at it, my heart starts beating. It's from Ja: *My mother says she dropped the folder. Sorry for leaving you in a fix I hope my Ma was okay. BTW, I have text Mr Edwards to give your name as my partner at the dance.*

Joyce is looking at me and because I am too shocked to speak, I hand her the phone. She squeals, 'You see! He was serious about going with you to the dance.' Joyce starts to gather all her belongings hurriedly. 'Let's go and buy fabric for your dress. You had better buy it today as it's only a week to the dance.

'I can't use that money.'

'Sula, do you want to go to the dance looking like Ja's partner or his housemaid?'

I keep quiet.

'Listen, do you want to die with nothing? I know you have brains but think about it. If Mr Helgesen hadn't offered to pay your school fees those brains of yours would have stayed here in Bellington because you would not have had the opportunity to study for your A levels which means no university scholarship to study abroad.'

'What do my brains have to do with taking stolen money?'

'It's about the way you think. You want to go to the dance and you want Ja to like you. How will that happen? You need to have a dress to wear and you have to look nice. How do you expect that to happen without money?' Joyce waits for her words to sink in, then hugs me. 'Trust me, you are going to go to the dance and you'll be the most beautiful girl in the hall. I will make sure of that.'

I remain quiet. She has a point. There's nothing I want more than to go to the dance looking beautiful and as Ja's partner, but I can't get my mind off the green bag that is bulging in the plastic bag she has tucked under her arm. Joyce says we have to go. She takes my hand. As she reaches for the door, I take the bag from her and zip it into my laptop bag, because the bulge is too conspicuous in the plastic bag and we don't want it catching Amake Miriam's eagle eye. Joyce smiles, my action has confirmed I'm with her. We hurry out the room and straight into Amake Miriam. She asks us to sit down in the living room and wait as she dials a number and speaks into the phone. 'The girls are ready. I will send them over now.' When she hangs up she says, 'Take a taxi straight to Lukeke Chambers. Miriam wants to speak to you.' We smile, nod, and thank her, then leave.

When we exit the gate Joyce bursts into a string of cuss words but when she flags down the taxi, she says, 'Lukeke Chambers.' Even with all her defiance, she cannot dare disobey Amake Miriam.

My heart sinks because my plan was to buy the fabric and get back to working on my project by lunchtime. But the detour via Lukeke Chambers, for what we both know is a sermon by Amake Miriam's lawyer daughter, means it is unlikely I'll be home by lunchtime as I'd hoped. Joyce senses I'm despondent because she tells me not to worry. She reminds me of the secret to dealing with the long sermons adults are fond of giving. 'Just keep very quiet and keep your head bowed. She'll tire of the sound of her own voice and she'll shut it. Then we can get on with our lives,' Joyce says.

I don't say anything. Joyce should know, she has heard enough sermons in her life to be an expert.

Lukeke Chambers is an old colonial style house re-modelled into law chambers. The walls are white, the grass very green, the wooden floors shine like mirrors. It is one of those places that make you feel out of place. The man at the reception waves us up the carpeted stairs and at the top we find Miriam Lukeke standing on the landing, her elbow rested on the banister. I know her because she's always on TV and in the papers. I also remember seeing her around when she lived with her parents but I was about five years old then.

She greets us with a 'Hi' and opens her office door for us to follow her in. The letters LLB LLM are stencilled in black after her name on the wooden door. Joyce enters first, I follow behind. Miriam Lukeke is a big, broad shouldered woman with sharp narrow hips. She looks like a man from behind. She has pitch black skin and long dreadlocks that fall halfway down her back. Today her big body is squashed into a pair of black jeans and a tight white tee shirt.

'Hello young ladies,' she says, smiles and pulls back the two chairs before her desk for us to sit on. 'We do not work Saturdays so I am just in to catch up on stuff,' she says to explain her casual dress. She abruptly switches off her smile as she sits down behind her desk facing us.

'Look at you,' she says to Joyce. 'Look at what this man has done to your pretty face.' The room falls silent. 'And I bet this is not the first time.'

Joyce nods. 'He is very jealous.'

'Is it the last time?'

Joyce folds her hands in her lap and bows her head in response.

'If you're not careful the next time he beats you up you'll end up like this.' Miriam walks over to a chest of drawers and with her foot yanks open the lowest drawer. From it she pulls out a rumpled black plastic bag. 'Do you know what this is?' she asks us both, shaking the bag open and laying it on the thick red carpet. The bag has a zip straight down the middle. 'This is a body bag for dead bodies. And if you, young lady, stay with the man who rearranged your face like that, you will end up in this!'

Joyce looks up.

'Come here.' Miriam snaps.

Joyce gets up and walks up to Miriam who pulls off her trainers. She then unzips the bag and steps into it. 'I want you to zip me up in this.' She lies down flat on her back.

Joyce hesitates.

'Go on.'

Joyce bends to her knees and starts zipping up the bag slowly. When the zip gets up to Miriam's neck, Joyce stops.

'Zip it up!'

Joyce seems to fumble with the zipper, for her hands are shaking. I start to breathe fast, my heart beating.

'If you don't leave that man. This will be you,' Miriam says. 'And your mother will be zipping up the bag after she has identified you. And imagine how she will feel. How would you feel if you ever had to zip up your daughter because she was too weak to walk away from an abusive man?' Miriam pushes her arms out of the bag to unzip it. She jumps to her feet and kicks the bag away. 'I am not trying to scare you young ladies. But the reality is that women die every day from physical abuse by their partners. A lot of women die from domestic violence.'

Joyce and I don't say anything. Miriam goes on, 'I used to be in one, you know? An abusive relationship. I used to keep him in my house and feed him and on top of that I gave him an added bonus; the privilege of using me as a punching bag so he could relieve himself of his frustrations. Until one day I woke up in a hospital bed and I didn't know what day of the week it was.'

Miriam carries on talking as the man from the reception comes in with three bottles of Coca Cola and places a bottle each before us. Miriam still carries on not minding that he hears her call herself a fool.

'And he was frustrated because I was more successful than he was. If I had not left I would have died. Ended up in that.' She points at the discarded body bag. 'How much money does he pay for your rent and how much pocket money does he give you?' Before Joyce can work it out, Miriam goes on still, 'Do you know that if you lived at your parents' house and cut down on all the expensive hair and clothes, you could use the money he gives you to educate yourself?'

Then after staring at Joyce and then me for a few silent minutes that make me feel like I am shrinking, Miriam finally smiles again. I think it's a sign that she is through with her talk.

Joyce looks up and says, 'I won't go back.'

Miriam chuckles, more like a snort, then apes a deep gruff voice and says, 'Honey, I don't know what came over me. I hate myself for abusing you. I love you and our daughter. I can't live without you. Please come back.'

There is a silence in the room before Joyce says, 'I am leaving him because I don't want to end up in a body bag.'

In her usual voice Miriam says, 'I want to believe you but I have seen too many women go back.'

Joyce says in a louder voice, 'I don't want to end up in a body bag!'

Miriam's smile is wry, but it creases the sides of her mouth. She sighs, then reaches for a box on her desk, and hands her business card to Joyce and me. 'Call me whenever you're in trouble. But remember I can only help you if you really want to help yourself.' She turns to me and says she hopes I was listening. That she doesn't want to ever hear that a man has used my face as a punching bag. Then she calls her driver from her mobile and asks him to drop us off.

As we are being chauffeured in Miriam's shiny black Mercedes, Joyce says, 'She doesn't believe me. She thinks like most women I'll be back again with a bruised face or in a body bag.' Then, sinking back into the soft white leather, Joyce smiles and says, 'What she doesn't know is that I am not like other women. I am Joyce. And when I say I am out of Mo's life I mean it. I have a plan.'

She is gazing out the window as if musing out loud to herself but the triumphant smirk on her face when she speaks causes the hairs on the back of my neck to stand up.

Chapter 8

Ja

My phone breaks apart as it smashes to the floor. A little boy I hadn't noticed earlier jumps, clutches the side of his face and yelps. A shard has caught him. I reach out to him to apologise. He looks at me wide-eyed and totters away crying. I run after him. He thinks I'm chasing him so he runs faster; I follow him asking him to stop. He runs up to a bench where a woman is sitting breastfeeding a baby.

'I am so sorry. I hurt him by mistake.' I explain pointing at her son.

She nods at me uninterested and asks her son to sit by her. I have a roll of mint sweets in my pocket so I pull it out and hand it to the boy. His face lights up. The mother thanks me. I walk away still apologising. Shame burns in my face. How can I lose control of myself in front of all these people? I imagine what I must look like to them; a spoilt boy screaming because his father is unwell. Most of them have been queuing for hours, on empty stomachs after walking for miles to get to the clinic and they are not screaming and shouting.

George finds me picking up the pieces of my phone. He comes up to me and leads me by the elbow to the Toyota Hilux. He has obviously heard about my tantrum. I've figured that word spreads faster than light in this place. They all know who I am. My face burns even hotter at the thought.

'Let us go now. The old man is sleeping anyway. We'll come back tomorrow.' I sense George is making up the bit about my father sleeping, but I don't say anything. I let him open the car door for me; I get in like a sulky child. As we drive out of the hospital I keep my head down. I am too ashamed to look up at the people I feel staring at me.

George drives in silence. I wonder what he makes of my childish tantrums. Or what he thinks of me. He turns into an enclosure, only to stop by a bottle store. He parks alongside three cars already stationed there. He says he'll be back and jumps out of the car. Two young men, each with a beer bottle in hand, are seated on the bonnet of the white Mazda closest to our Hilux. They have obviously parked there a while, for they are having a loud animated conversation, punctured by high fiving, sparring and fits of laughter. Next to the Madza is a blue jeep. It's surrounded by three young women who are engaged in conversation with the male occupants of the car. I cannot see the model of the red car on the other side of the jeep or who is inside, but I see a fourth woman standing by the window on the passenger side talking to whoever is in the car.

George comes out of the bottle store, and one of the young ladies says something to him. His response must have sounded funny, for the girls crack up laughing. George gets in the car and hands me a bottle of beer.

'There's always a first time,' he says noting my hesitation.

'Why not.' I utter my first words since we left the hospital. I take a gulp from the bottle. I have known the taste of beer from when I was a child and my papa would give me sips from his glass. The effects of alcohol I have only started to know and appreciate more recently. Tiger and I have made a habit of helping ourselves to his Dad's liquor cabinet.

A few gulps from my bottle and I start to feel my head grow lighter and the tingling in my knees.

'Slow down,' George says when I take another swig. 'I'm meant to be a good influence on you, remember?'

'Yeah, I'll stick by you. Because this sucker's had enough bad influences in his life,' I reply.

'Your Dad's a nice guy, you know. I know he made some bad choices but I have come to know him. He's a good guy.'

'Tell that to my mother and her parents.'

George shrugs then says, 'I'm not here to point fingers. All I'm saying is what is done is done. What we need to do is move from here. And remember, no matter what, he's still your Dad.'

'The guy's dying. He and I aren't going to be moving much further than this.' I surprise myself at the way I face up to the fact that my old man is dying. Then I surprise myself even more by confessing, 'You know when I was young I used to tell people he was dead. Just so that I didn't have to admit to myself or anyone that he was alive but didn't care enough to defy my grandparents and come see me.'

'You know, what happened between your parents happened. Try not to take sides. It's not easy but do look at it through your own lenses.' George wipes the moisture off the bottle with the inside of his tee shirt. 'Your parents were young and different.'

'My grandparents didn't like him.' As an afterthought I say, 'He didn't fit in.'

We turn to watch the two young women move from car to car entertaining the occupants. Perhaps they are being entertained by the car owners. A fifth woman appears and joins them, she looks to be on the plump side, her lips painted pink, and an NYC baseball cap on her head. She goes into the bottle store, turns on the music, steps back on to the verandah where she starts to wiggle her backside. We have no choice but to watch and she seems very aware of it. She moves her round hips in gyrating motions. Her body sways up and down, then side to side. She is wearing tight fitting white jeans so every movement of her body seems pronounced. She turns her back to us, and I see that the top of her black underwear is showing above her low waist jeans. Something about her height and build reminds me of Sula and I wonder if she has finished the project. To distract myself I say, 'She reminds me of a girl in my class.'

'A girl you like?'

'No. Sula. My lab partner.'

George laughs. 'You said that *No* quick. It's all right to like a girl.'

'I don't like her in that way. She's just my lab partner.'

'Okay. But ask yourself why this girl dancing here has got you thinking of your lab partner.'

I decide not to take the conversation with George any further. One of the slim girls, who appears caught up in a conversation by the red car, now jumps onto the verandah and starts to dance as well. She has on a short pink dress with purple cycling shorts underneath. The girls move close to each other and jiggle their hips in time.

'They know what they're doing,' George says. 'I think it's time for another drink.' He slides out of the car and leaves me to watch the girls.

I watch the girls dance, the slim one looks straight at me and beams me a smile. I look away quickly. George comes out of the bar with five beers, and says something to the girls as he walks to the car. I reach across and open the door for him. The slim girl struts up to my window. As she is approaching, George hands me four bottles and says, 'Give her three.'

I hand the drinks to the girl through the window. She has on a very strong perfume that catches in my throat. She smiles at me, takes two beers, and says she will be back for the third. She takes her time strutting away, then makes her way back to the car. When

I hand her the bottle she takes a swig and asks, 'What's your name?'

'Ja.'

'My name is Pearl. You are fine.' She winks at me, then with a smile she climbs back onto the verandah and continues to dance with the bottle in her hand.

'The invitation has been made.' George prompts me with a chuckle. 'It's up to you to take it or leave it.'

My heartbeat quickens and because I don't know what to say or do, I take a long swig from my beer.

We spend a while at Kaba's. Cars drive out and others drive in. The girls also change. The sun sets. At some stage we get out of the car and sit on the ledge of the verandah. A work colleague of George joins us. I lose sense of time. At some point the Sula lookalike who had disappeared re-appears without the cap and the white jeans. She is wearing black leggings and a while halter neck top. She sits beside me and we have a conversation about alcohol, or is it music? I can't recall. Her artificial nails are painted different colours, blue, green and yellow and I wonder why, although I don't ask. She wears a silver ring, shaped like a spider, on her middle finger. Next thing I know George is dancing on the verandah with Pearl who has changed into a white dress. She stops dancing, comes over, and sits with me. She tells me she only went home to shower because she felt hot and sweaty.

We drink more beers and eat chicken grilled over charcoal. It's hot from the heat and the spices, but it's soft and tasty. The skin is crisp. Chicken has never tasted so good. At some point I realise my lips have gone all numb. And I decide I can't drink anymore.

Soon after, George says it's time to leave. As we walk to his car I notice that Pearl and the Sula lookalike are coming with us. I don't say anything. George drives to his place. He tells me it's his place as he parks. I can't see much so I follow him blindly. I stumble and giggle. Pearl takes hold of my hand and giggles with me. We enter the dark apartment. The power is out. George announces that he forgot to buy some fuel for the generator.

I make out a couch and collapse on it, if only to stop myself falling over, the room is spinning. The girls ask George where the bathroom is and disappear giggling. George quickly squeezes something rubbery into my hand. 'Your life depends on this,' he says.

I realise it is a condom and start to protest. 'I don't know, I've never-'

'Don't worry, it's instinct,' George reassures me quietly. 'It's like eating. You don't need to be taught. And trust me she knows what she's doing.' He disappears before I can ask any more questions. Then I hear him dragging one of the giggling girls away. The other joins me on the sofa. It's Pearl. She tells me to relax.

'Don't worry sweetie,' she whispers into my face. 'I will take good care of you. You're fine.'

So I keep quiet. She does things to me that make me forget about Ma. I forget about my old man and his kidney. I forget about Sula and the science project. And I discover that George was wrong; it is nothing like eating. It's one hundred times better.

Chapter 9

Sula

It's a Saturday and the end of the month so people are out spending their salaries. The city centre is packed with humans stepping over one another like crabs in a bucket. Joyce takes my hand to make sure I stay with her. I try not to think about the money in my bag but whenever I spot a police officer my heart jumps. I keep my fear and guilt to myself.

The inside of the fabric shop is warm enough to bake a cake and because I haven't eaten breakfast I start feeling lightheaded. Joyce takes her time scouring through the satin fabrics. She points out bales of fabric and the shop assistant's expression turns increasingly sour as he loads and unloads bales of cloth off the shelves to Joyce's instructions. Everyone is looking at her face but Joyce seems oblivious to the attention her blue lip and purple eye are causing. She reels fabric off each bale to the length of her bruised arm and holds it against me to see if the colour compliments my skin tone. Then she feels the fabric with her cheek. Eventually we're down to a deep purple or a rust colour similar to that of a new copper coin. I choose the rust because it is unusual. Joyce agrees with my choice. Only then I admit that I feel faint and Joyce pays for the fabric and she rushes me out of the shop.

It is noon already. I start to panic. I know the Internet cafe opens till 8 p.m. but I have to be home by 6.30 p.m. (Bambo's directive) so I only have about five hours. To add to my woes, Joyce suggests we go to the second-hand clothes market so that I can buy a pair of shoes and a handbag to match. I want to tell her I don't have the time, that I have to do the project if it is to be ready for submission on Monday, but her enthusiasm discourages me from saying anything. After all, she is doing it all for me. She buys some Fanta orange and chicken pies and we head for a stall that belongs to a friend of hers. We eat as we sift through piles of shoes and handbags. There are row upon row of shoes bound together with rubber bands.

Finally, at 2.30 p.m. we make our purchase. Before we part company Joyce gives me a pep talk. She is certain that I will look great at the dance. Then she tells me not to feel intimidated by Ja. 'He is human like you,' she says. Staring briefly into my eyes, she tells me not to worry or feel guilty about her and the money because she has a plan and that everything will soon be okay.

I set off for the Internet café armed with my new fabric, pair of stain chocolate colour heels, a matching clutch bag and guilt for having used some of the stolen money. I keep running Joyce's words in my words to relieve some of the guilt. Having tried on the sandals I doubt I will be able to walk in them, but Joyce insisted they looked great on my feet and with practice I would be fine. As I make my way to the Internet café I admit to myself that my excitement at my shopping is starting to override my panic about the project. I imagine myself in a dress and the shoes, and my mind becomes filled with different ways I could style my hair. The thoughts fill my head until I get to my stop and have to alight from the bus.

Fortunately, being a Saturday afternoon, the Internet café is not busy so I find a free PC and start typing furiously. I copy the notes and data from the sheets of paper onto the document, and then I lift the charts and diagrams off the usb and paste them into the document. I work nonstop, as quickly as I can. But before I know it, it is 6.12 p.m. I log off, only to discover that the cafe printer is out of colour ink. The owner says they will buy the ink first thing on Monday morning. He says the cafe does not open on Sundays. I think of printing the project in black and white but I realise it won't really work since our charts and diagrams are colour coded. To print in black and white I would have to use shading and that would take time. As I ponder my desperate situation, Amai calls to ask me to hurry home because Bambo has just asked after me and she has told him that I had called to say I was stuck in traffic. When I explain my situation Amai says I can try and find another Internet cafe that opens on Sunday. I grab my goods. I decide to spend some of the money Joyce gave me to book a taxi home so I can get there quickly. When I get home Bambo is on the verandah. The sun has set but when I stand before him I know he is looking at my shopping bags.

'Your mother said you were at the Internet cafe working.'

'Yes Bambo. I was doing my project.'

'The same project your friend's mother came here about.'

'Yes Bambo.'

'And those shopping bags are they part of the project?'

'No Bambo. This is fabric I bought for my dress to wear to the dance.'

'Have you finished your project work?'

'No Bambo.

'So why are you out shopping for dresses?'

'I have almost finished.'

'The dance is a week from today. The project is due the day after tomorrow and you're telling me that you have almost finished your project. Almost?'

'The project is due by 5 p.m. on Monday. I have finished, I just needed to print but the colour printer was out of ink. So I will go out and print it tomorrow.'

'And church?'

'I will go after church.'

'Are you sure all that is left is to print?'

'Yes Bambo.'

'Then bring your usb. I will print it for you tomorrow. You can't afford to miss the submission deadline. Don't follow that lab partner of yours and his fancy mother. If he fails or is kicked out of school his mother will pay to send him somewhere else. If you're kicked out; that's it.'

'Please Bambo, leave the child alone. She has been out working all day. She left before the sun was up.' Amai steps out on the verandah. Amai Mukulu also materializes from the back of the house but she doesn't say anything. She is just there to show Amai moral support. I feel bad that Amai is protecting me. What would she do if she knew I had used stolen money to buy the fabric? She must have assumed I used some of the monthly allowance I get from Mr Helgesen.

'So school work involves shopping?'

Amai and Amai Mukulu look at my shopping bags. I know I should say something but I don't. I can't say Joyce bought the fabric for me as that will surely give her away. So I keep quiet.

'You went shopping?' Amai Mukulu asks

'I just bought some fabric for my dress. '

'Forget the dress. Forget the dance,' Bambo says. 'It is distracting you from your school work.

'Let the child go to ' Amai starts to say but stops because Bambo cuts in:

'Give me your usb so I can print the thing for you tomorrow.'

I start to fumble in my bag for my usb. Then a sinking feeling starts in my stomach, I feel as if all my insides have deflated. I look up at Bambo. And as the reality of what has happened washes over me, I say, 'I think I've have left the usb at the Internet cafe.'

'Aha, Ha!' Bambo says to the Amai, 'You see? Is she serious about her work? She has left the usb at the cafe but she remembered to carry the clothes because her mind is on the Dance.' Bambo turns to me. 'Listen here. And Listen carefully. You are not going to that dance.'

Chapter 10

Ja

Someone shakes me violently and I hear myself shout as I jolt out of deep sleep. My eyes spring open and I find myself staring into George's eyes. He clamps his hand over my mouth until he is sure I am fully awake. As I come to, I take in George's living-room in full daylight, the sofa that I am lying on and two plastic garden chairs, a wooden display cabinet with nothing in it and a new Panasonic 32-inch plasma in the corner. My mouth tastes as if it is full of flour. My bladder feels as if it's about to burst. There is a loud banging on the door. I recognise it as the sound that has been pounding in my ears and penetrating my sleep. Whoever it is must have been knocking for a while.

A female voice calls out, 'George!'

'Auntie Jean,' George mouths. I jump to my feet. George puts his index finger to his lips, signalling I stay quiet. I pull on my jeans as quickly and quietly as I can.

As I buckle my belt and reach for my tee shirt and jacket, George whizzes around the room, picks two beer bottles off the floor and shoves them in the display cabinet drawer; one still has beer in it so when he closes the drawer a trail of frothy beer cascades down the front of the wooden unit and starts to puddle on the floor. George notices but it is the least of his worries. He picks the bedspread off the sofa and flings it out the room into the corridor, then shuts the door. I pick the condom wrapper off the floor, but George grabs it out of my hands and stuffs it in the back pocket of his jeans. It all happens in a few seconds and all the while Auntie is banging on the door.

I am wondering where the girls have gone. George must

have read my thoughts because he whispers, 'They've gone out the back door.' Then he looks me over, pulls chewing gum out of his pocket, pops one in his mouth and tosses the packet to me. We scan the room a final time. Then George turns to open the front door.

Auntie Jean bursts in, her eyes ablaze. 'George, what is going on here?'

'Hello Auntie,' George says with a wide smile as if he hasn't noticed Auntie Jean's anger or the fact that she has been banging on the door for several minutes. He steps out of the living room onto the verandah so Auntie Jean is forced to follow him back out. 'I took Ja to see the work we are doing then we went to have a drink and some food,' George says. 'It got a bit late so I thought other than disturb you, he should spend the night here with me.'

'But why didn't you call? His mother has been calling because she says his phone is off. His father is also very worried because he didn't come back home.'

I decide to say something. 'It's my fault, Auntie Jean. My phone stopped working yesterday so that's why my mother could not get hold of me.' I start to feel my pockets. I try to recall where my phone is. The chewing gum is not doing much to counter the sour taste in my mouth and my head is pounding. I try to sound as clear and chirpy as George.

He volunteers to drive me to the hospital so we can explain to my father but Aunt Jean is not having any of it. She says she will take me in her brother's car to the hospital. It is obvious she does not want me alone with George. He rushes off to his car and comes back with parts of my phone; he manages to put them back together and switches it on. I thank him, say a quick goodbye and walk to the waiting car with Aunt Jean.

As we drive off I turn to look at George. He has a serious face, but he raises his eyebrows, gives me a discreet thumbs-up, then mouths, 'I'll call.'

Aunt jean and the driver who I assume is her brother are quiet all the way to the hospital. Thank god because I use the time to contemplate the previous twenty-four hours, too many things have happened. I have met my younger brother, offered my kidney up to my father, struck up a friendship with George and landed up in his house with a strange woman I will probably never see again. My thoughts, and visions, and feelings of the last twenty-four hours are all jumbled in with the throbbing going on in my head.

We get to the hospital and with no words exchanged I get out and follow the driver to the ward. Aunt jean remains in the car. When we get to the door, the man opens it for me to go in, but he remains outside. I wonder if he is there to guard me. Aunt Jean obviously does not trust me anymore.

The old man looks much better than yesterday and I'm not sure if it is because I am over the initial shock of seeing him unwell. He smiles at me. 'Your mother has been looking for you. She has called me eleven times this morning.' His smile is weary.

I have to smile back before I turn serious and apologise for causing everyone so much trouble.

He shrugs. 'So did you boys have a good time?'

'It was okay.' I try to play it down. My throat is dry but I know water is scarce in the hospital so I try to keep my eyes off the bottle of still water sitting in a basket by the bedside. My father must have read my mind because he asks me if I would like some water. I wonder whether he can tell just by looking at me that I spent most of the previous day drinking. He has done it before so he must know what it is like. I decline his offer because I think it is the honourable thing to do. If only to prove to myself that after my conduct over the last twenty-four hours I have an ounce of honour left in me.

'Your mother was concerned that something might have happened to you. I explained that it's a small place so if anything happened to you I would know.'

I look down. I can't help but feel that he knows exactly what I was up to the night before.

'She was very worried that you had decided to help me get better?' he says in the tone of a question. Before I can say anything he goes on, 'I have lived a long full life. And when God decides it's time for me to go it will be time for me to go. I don't think it's my time now. I feel better. I know I'm recovering so don't worry about me. Focus on working hard in school. Applying yourself to your full potential in everything you do and making your mother proud.'

I remain quiet and wait for him to tell me to be a good boy because hell, after last night I need it. But he doesn't go there. He asks me to respect my mother because she has given me the best of everything. And that even when I don't agree with her I should remember she cares and chances are that in a few years' time I will understand where she was coming come. When he is through he says I had better leave since it is a long trip back home. As I shake his hand he grabs hold of it with both of his and says, 'Remember son, it's often easier to mess up than to do good.' Then he opens out his arms to me for a quick embrace before he releases me and settles back onto the bed.

An hour and a half later, I am back at my old man's house packing my small bag. I manage to convince Auntie Jean's younger brother to stop at the small shopping centre. He shows me where I could get some jeans for Eric. Fortunately my wallet is still in my jeans. I buy Eric a pair of jeans, two shirts and a baseball cap and I pick up a couple of denim skirts and tee shirts for the girls. Auntie Jean's brother helped me with the sizes. Back at the house the kids are running around me excitedly after receiving their gifts. Eric is beaming as I have also given him my baseball cap which he seems to prefer over the one I just bought him. Mwati arrives just as I finish packing. After waving goodbye to Aunt Jean and the kids I settle in the back of the car. I am looking forward to the four-hour-drive ahead of me. I need to think. But Ma has other ideas. My phone starts ringing as soon as we get on to the main road.

I start to give a quick apology for not calling her, for having my phone off. But as ever, she surprises me. She doesn't ask where I was the night before. Her first question is, 'Is it true that you have invited that girl from Bellington to the dance have you gone crazy?'

Chapter 11

Sula

I spend Sunday avoiding Bambo. He is walking around talking to himself and loudly asking God what he has done to deserve such useless daughters. Each time he asks such rhetorical questions Zafika will quip, 'Except me Bambo. I am not useless.' To which Bambo will say he is relying on her to salvage his name, 'Because your sisters are intent on putting my name to shame.'

I am not the only one irritated with Zafika; at some point while Bambo is talking, Amai Mukulu mutters, 'If you don't stop running that mouth of yours I will stop it for you.' And that turns Zafika's running mouth off and into a pout.

I don't pay Bambo or Zafika or anyone else much attention, my mind is occupied. On the one hand, I am trying to convince myself that if Ja's usb is lost I can put together a new report in four hours. The report is due in at noon. So if the usb is lost I will have to redo parts of it. I have some information on my usb but I will still need input from Ja. I hope he saved the charts on his laptop as well as on his usb. Now I have to deal with telling him that I have lost his usb. After a while I decide to call him, the sooner he knows the better. My heart thumps as I dial but my call goes straight to his voice mail. I take a deep breath and leave a message. 'This is Sula. I have misplaced your usb. I can get the report done by noon tomorrow which is Monday but I need some information from you.' The phone bleeps and cuts because I take too long to leave a message so I call again. This time I tell him to meet me at the Internet café in the mall, and then I cut the line. For some reason, I feel like a weight has been lifted off my shoulders. At least now I have told him, all I can do is wait for him to get back to me.

After dinner Amai Mukulu knocks on the door and enters my bedroom with the big green book she writes her client's measurements in and a measuring tape tied around her ample waist. She finds me sketching out how I will reassemble the project in case the usb is lost. She asks me if I still want to go to the dance. Although I am devastated about Bambo banning me from going to the dance, a part of me is relieved because at least this way I don't get to find out whether or not Ja was serious about inviting me. At least now when I tell him I am unable to go to the dance I will be telling the truth.

I tell Amai Mukulu that I will not be going to the dance because Bambo has forbidden me.

'That is not my question.' Amai Mukulu explains that Bambo will be out of town and she and Amai feel that I have not done anything to warrant being banned so they will allow me to go.

Her words fill me with hope and apprehension in equal measure. I am not sure what to say. She misreads my hesitation again. 'Don't worry; if Bambo ever finds out, we will tell him that we granted you permission.'

I smile.

'What is the matter?'

'I am still not sure if I have a partner to go with to the dance.'

'But didn't he ask you?'

I nod.

'So why aren't you sure?'

'He might have been joking. Maybe he asked to make fun of me?'

' Is he cruel to you or has he been horrible to you before?

I shake my head.

'So?'

Before I can say anything Amai Mukulu opens her book and

asks me to stand up straight. 'Let me take your measurements,' she says in a tone that suggests I have no say in the matter.

The next morning I check my phone and find a message from Ja that he will be at the mall by 7.30 a.m. My stomach tightens from anxiety. I find myself taking extra care while getting ready. It takes me ages to decide what to wear. Ja has only ever seen me in uniform. After several changes of outfits, I eventually settle for dark skinny jeans and a gold knitted twin set, a sleeveless vest with a matching cropped cardigan that Joyce gave to me but I have never worn. It is one of those expensive tops where the labels are attached to the garment with a pretty ribbon.

The mall car park is still empty when I arrive so I spot Ja leaning against his mother's car right away. I feel self- conscious as I walk towards him. I don't know if I should look at him or whether to smile or wave. In the end I just walk towards him without looking at his face, though mine feels as if it is on fire. When I get closer he walks towards me. He is smiling, which is a relief, given that I might have lost his usb. He seems to have forgotten that I called him a mummy's baby.

To hide how nervous I feel, I say a quick hello and start listing our options if we end up not finding the usb.

He asks me to calm down, which makes me feel silly, even more nervous. We sit on a bench outside the café since it has not yet opened for business. Ja suggests we ask for an extension if we can't find the usb other than hand in a hurriedly put together project.

Bambo's words ring in my ears. Ja might be able to get away with asking for an extension, I certainly wouldn't. Bambo would kill me. Besides if word got to Mr Helgesen that I was submitting work in late he might think I don't appreciate his sponsorship. Of course I don't say this to Ja. Instead I say, 'Fingers crossed, the usb is there. And if it isn't we have six hours to do it. The information is there, all we need do is to put it together again and add in a few details here and there.'

I think he hears the determination in my voice so he doesn't push the extension deadline thing. Instead he says, 'If the usb is there we can go and print out the report at my house. Ma is not at home and my printer is fast.'

I change the subject because I am not sure how I feel about going to his house. I ask him why he wasn't at school on Friday. He tells me he went to see his sick father. He doesn't say anymore and because I know, everybody knows, that he doesn't live with his father, I sense there is an issue there. So I don't say anything.

He says, 'So you sing hey? My Ma said you were going for choir practice when she brought the folder.'

'Sometimes.' I wonder what else his Ma said about me and my family.

'Sing something.'

I'm not sure I heard him right. I look at him.

He smiles. 'Are you shy?'

'I sing gospel.'

'So? Sing gospel.'

'Here? In the middle of the street? Are you crazy?'

'So? Do you only sing on stage?'

'People will stare.'

'Okay. But you will sing, right? Remember we're going to my house. No one is there. Just you and me. So no excuses.'

I nod and smile because I know if I speak I will stammer. I start to feel sweaty in my palms and under my cardigan. I know I look smart in my cardigan but I wish I had put on something cooler. I recognise one of the Internet cafe staff getting off a bus across the road, and I feel relieved. I point him out to Ja.

He trots towards us. When he spots me he starts shaking his head. 'Sorry no ink,' he says. 'I will go to buy it now when my colleague comes.'

I tell him I have come to look for my usb. He says he hasn't seen it. He unlocks the grill gates and opens the main door. We find the usb in the monitor I had used and I almost pass out with relief. The feeling doesn't last because a few minutes later we are out of the café and heading for Ja's car. He opens the back door for me and I climb in. Then he jumps into the front and tells the driver that we are going back to his house.

The driver does not say anything, which in a way makes me feel uncomfortable. But Ja carries on as if it is just the two of us in the car. He asks me a question that throws me off guard.

'Do you have any brothers or sisters?'

'Two sisters. One older and the other younger.'

'I have one brother and two sisters, all younger than me.'

I am stunned by his words although I try to hide it. Everyone knows Ja is an only child. After a few minutes as if reading my mind he adds, 'They are my siblings on my father's side.'

Ja lives in one of those houses that look like a picture advertising luxury homes. There is a clear colour scheme, royal blue and cream in the cushions, the curtains, the sofa, the rugs and the abstract pictures on the wall. A small pool filled with clear blue water sits some metres away from the glass living room doors. He offers me a drink which I turn down as I try not to stare around at the inside of his house. Ja asks me to follow him into his bedroom. As I walk across the carpet I feel like apologising for stepping on it. Ja's bedroom is less intimidating, maybe because of the posters and the basketball net attached to the wall. I notice the two guitars on their stands in one corner of the room. There is a glass partitioning which Ja slides open, to reveal a desktop computer near the window. He offers me a chair and flurries about turning on the computer. We spend another hour and a half printing and collating documents. We then talk about what we will be doing after the exams. He says he will spend his holiday in Sempa with his siblings and his father as he waits for his results. He tells me he has just met them but wants to get to know them all better.

'My younger brother needs an elder brother to keep him in check,' Ja says, with a smile. And then he asks about my sisters.

I say, 'I have a beautiful elder sister who needs a younger sister to keep her in check and a cheeky younger sister who needs an elder sister to keep her in check.'

Ja laughs heartily. 'Sounds like you have a lot on your hands.'

As we head out of the house we hear a car and Ja says his Mum is home for lunch. My heart starts bumping against my chest. Ja notices because he smiles and says, 'Contrary to public opinion she doesn't bite.'

I try to smile but I suddenly feel out of breath. My throat becomes parched . Ja takes the report from me, asks, 'Are you okay?' I nod again. I take a deep breath and feel sweat beads burst through my pores. I don't have time enough to compose myself for the door to the landing where we are standing swings open.

'Ja - oh, sorry. I didn't realise you were with someone.' Ja's mother stands still. Her eyes sweep over us: Ja and I are standing close, the folder he was trying to retrieve from me, between us.

'We're just leaving,' Ja says, striding towards the door.

His mother is standing in the doorway so I decide not to tag along. I can't squeeze past her like he can. She looks me up and down. I say hello and she says hello back. I see she is sizing me up. Thank God, I have on an expensive top. She won't think too poorly of me.

As if reading my mind she says, 'You're the girl from Bellington, right? You look different. I like your top.' She moves out of the way.

I say a polite thank you ma, then a goodbye, and I walk past her. We head for the car but she calls Ja back. I don't know what she tells him but he slams the kitchen door and shouts something as he comes back out of the house and towards the car. I wonder how he can be so rude to his mother. For a moment I feel sorry for her.

The driver shakes his head and mutters, 'Aaa!....this boy is becoming a big problem.'

Ja jumps into the car and his mood changes. He turns and grins at me. 'Damn! I knew there was something I had forgotten,' he says. 'You were meant to sing for me! Anyway, there'll be another time.'

I am taken aback at how soon he recovers from his outburst with his mother. Her impact on me has not been quite so unmemorable. I feel giddy but perhaps it has less to do with facing his mother and more to do with the fact that he is entertaining the possibility of spending more time with me.

Ja doesn't leave me alone. He begs me to sing something as we drive to school. 'Just one line, please.'

I tell him I will sing, only if he sings first. He surprises me by breaking into an out of tune rendition of Tuface Idibia's *My African Queen*. It is so bad I burst out laughing. The driver laughs and offers to switch on the music, so we don't have to suffer ear pains. Ja then turns serious and says, 'Actually I do sing sometimes when I play the guitar.' He breathes in deeply and sings the first two lines of *Tears in Heaven* by Eric Clapton. I feel the hair stand up on the back of my neck. I'm still staring at him as the chill subsides inside me when he says, 'See! Told you I could sing. So now it's your turn.'

I know if I hesitate my nerves will get the better of me. So I take a deep breath and start singing *And I am telling* you from the musical *Dream Girls.* I sing the first verse but just before I sing the words *You're gonna love me*, I hesitate. The words hit me and I feel embarrassed at the words. The song comes out naturally because I have perfected it.

'This girl! You sing!' Ja's driver swings his head around to gape at me. My cheeks start to burn as it suddenly crosses my mind he might think I chose the song because of the significance of the words. I start trying to explain my choice of song but Ja cuts me short, 'Wow Sula - you can sing!' I can tell from the tone of his voice that he is genuinely impressed.

To hide my embarrassment I say, 'But...I told you...' Inside, I curse myself. Why didn't I sing *Amazing Grace* which is another song I've perfected?

Ja is staring at me and I can't hold my fake smile anymore. I stare back; for a moment, there is just the two us in the car. In fact, it feels as if there are just two of us in the whole wide world.

But the moment passes quickly because Mr Mwati sounds the horn and yells out a profanity at a woman who has just dashed across the road with a baby strapped to her back and a tray of groundnuts on her head. We don't recapture the moment as Mr Mwati takes the sharp turn just before the school gate and brakes suddenly. I see why he has stopped suddenly, Ja's gang is standing just outside the school wall. Lucy, in white jeans and a denim jacket, is leaning against the wall, while Tiger is sitting on the gate post, and Liseli and Kenya are reading something in a newspaper opened wide between them.

Just as suddenly as we are upon them, I see Ja change. He sits upright, his smile disappears. I sense our moment is not only lost but about to deteriorate so I quickly pick up my bag and the report and say, 'Thank you very much for the ride.' But before I push the door open the gang is upon us, surrounding the car and peering in through Mr Mwati's window.

'Where've you been, man?' Tiger asks and then I notice his next words catch in his throat when he sees me. He asks again, this time hesitantly, obviously disgusted by my presence, 'Where have you been?'

The girls' jaws drop open when they see me.

'Thank you, sir,' I say again to Mr Mwati and open the door. I don't look at Ja. But I push the door too hard, it swings open and almost knocks Lucy into the flower bed.

'Pardon me,' she says in a loud voice and I am forced to give a meek sorry in response. I get out of the jeep. In an effort to close the door, I push it back too hard and this time it slams shut.

Mr Mwati protests, 'Ah, careful!'

I mumble another sorry and stumble before I hurry off. I can feel them watching me. I hear Ja say something about the project. I hear Tiger say, 'Suuulala and Jaaaaa!' And I hear them all laugh. I hear car doors shutting and the car pulling away. As I turn into the reception area, I look back because they can't see me through the reception windows from outside. The car pulls away with the gang piled inside. I see Ja smiling. He doesn't even check to see if I have taken the folder or if it is still lying on the back seat of the car.

When I get home Amai Mukulu and Amai present me with my dress for the dance. I have to say it is more beautiful than I imagined. The top half of the dress is a sleeveless brocade fabric of gold, deep brown and rust. The bottom half is the rust satin fabric Joyce and I bought; it is fitted tight with a mermaid-like tail. I am speechless.

'You like it, don't you?' Amai says, making a face.

I am so pleased I hug them both. I can tell from their faces that they are as pleased as I am. They must have sat up and sewed all day. I try on the dress and act excited because I don't want to dampen everyone's spirits by telling them that Ja dumped me when he saw his friends. I will deal with all that later; for now I act like I am ready to go to the dance. Amai Mukulu lays some newspapers on the verandah so the dress doesn't get dirty and I twirl around for them before Amai Mukulu starts to place pins in places she wants to adjust. Zafika is prancing around excitedly and imitates me as she struts her own make-believe catwalk, then the gate opens and Bambo walks in. Silence descends.

'Eh he, what is this?' Bambo asks. 'Did I not say she is not going to the dance?'

I turn and hurry into the house to take off the dress.

I hear Amai say, 'Bambo, the child has submitted the report and- '

Bambo does not give Amai a chance to respond. He says he once had hope in me but his hopes are fading fast. He says he can see me coming home one day soon with a Letti of my own. But this time Amai does not let him go on.

She stands up and shouts back at him. 'How can the child succeed? When her father has no faith in her?' She says she's tired of him feeling sorry for himself. 'Sula gets the best grades in the whole school but instead of encouraging and hailing her you find the one, *ONE* occasion when she misplaces her usb and you make it the focus of your ranting. What sort of wet blanket are you?'

Bambo tries to shut her up, but Amai goes on defiantly. 'Sula is going to the dance. If she comes back pregnant I will look after the baby.' She says this at the top of her voice: Amai hardly says anything in more than a whisper so Bambo and the rest of us are stunned. Even Amai Mukulu looks shocked. And I realise I will have to go to the dance because Amai has stood up for me. To now say that I am not going to the dance would be to side with Bambo and I can't do that.

Bambo throws his hands in the air, appearing defeated, and announces that from now on he will not get involved in any business of the children in the house because today Amai has grown a beard and declared herself the man of the house. He says, 'You are now the mother and the father of this house.' To which Amai surprises everyone, no doubt Bambo included.

'Yes! I am the man of the house,' she replies. 'And as the man of the house I say, Sula is going to the dance!' And she sits down and starts making the adjustments to my dress.

Chapter 12

Ja

The first thing I do when I wake up Tuesday morning is check my phone. There is a message from Tiger: *Lucy whining coz u haven't asked her 2 the dance. She thinks u've invited Mercy.*'

I decide to reply to the text, although I am irritated that Tiger and everyone has assumed I will invite Lucy or Mercy. I have no messages from Sula, as I expected, she didn't respond to any of the seven texts I sent her yesterday so I don't know why I keep checking my phone. Not that I blame her. I don't know why I let her go and submit the folder alone, why I dashed off with the guys without even saying goodbye to her. Now I can't even dare ask her if she handed it in because really I should know it's half my responsibility. I want to talk to her and apologise for what I did but I'm stuck because I don't have an explanation except that I am a fool. I think of George and what he said about human beings falling into the trap of playing to the gallery.

If I'm honest, the only reason I haven't made friends with Sula over the past two years or why I am anxious about having invited her to the dance is because she doesn't fit. The same way my father didn't fit. With that thought fresh in my mind I pick up my phone and send a text to Tiger: *I have invited Sula to the dance so I cannot turn around. I have to take her*. I hit the 'send' button, then feel guilty because by saying I can't turn around it makes it sound obligatory on my part. Whereas the reality is that I invited Sula because I want to and because I enjoy her company. As I think about it, my mobile rings. It is George. He asks if we travelled safely and whether Ma gave me stick for having my phone off. He tells me my old man has been discharged. 'I think you coming to see him has a lot to do with his recovery. He will go back in for the operation at some point but the good thing is he's feeling and looking much better.'

George's words send a wave of relief through me. I thank him for calling and for checking up on my old man. In my euphoria I hear myself say that I will go back to Sempa for the holidays. My words are met with silence on the other end.

'Are you sure? I mean it will be nice of you to come spend time with your dad and his family, but this place is a dump. It's one thing to spend one night here but to stay for weeks?' George says.

I tell him I am sure I want to spend time with my old man. To convince him, I say that I will carry my gadgets with me so I can listen to music and have Internet access. George says he will be pleased to have me as company and wishes me good luck in the forthcoming exams before he hangs up.

Feeling charged from my conversation with George, I get up and find Ma in the TV room watching one of the many American reality TV shows she has become addicted to. Her handbag is in her lap and her car keys in her hand. She's dressed for work, in all green, including her tights and her shoes, such that to me she looks like a chameleon. The previous night when I got home from Sempa we kept the conversation light, no mention of donating kidneys or of Sula. We stuck to safe conversations such as the traffic on the road and how tired I was, to avoid a fight.

'So what's for today?' Ma asks and quickly adds, 'I am only asking because I wanted to give Mwati the day off after the long driving he did over the weekend. So you won't have transport today.'

'I plan to stay home all week and study,' I say and I see Ma's eyes light up. She asks me about my exam timetable and I fill her in. Then I decide to make use of her good mood. 'Ma, do you need the computer in the study. The desktop?'

'That's why it's there.'

'I know but there's a laptop and we have a desktop in my room.'

'We? I have them. You don't have anything?'

Okay. She has sensed something and decided she's going to make things hard for me. 'Okay,' I sigh. 'Do *you* need the desktop in the study?'

'Why?' Ma asks.

I go straight for the kill. 'I want to give it to Eric.'

'Who's Eric?'

I start to say my little brother but the look on Ma's face stops me, so instead I say, 'He's dad's son.'

Ma sighs. 'Ja, I know you have discovered family. But they are not your responsibility.'

'I have three computers at my disposal here. Eric has to walk and queue at an Internet cafe to do his homework. Isn't it natural that I would want to lend him one?'

'Lend? How do you expect to get it back? At what stage will he have no use for it?' Ma asks. 'Bobo, I appreciate you wanting to help. But be warned; once you start giving you have opened the floodgates. You are still young. Do you want to commit yourself to supporting your siblings even before you start working or have a family of your own? The reality is that once you start there is no turning back. It's a normal reaction to want to help, but as your mother I want you to understand what you are letting yourself in for. You can't wake up in two years' time and say I've done enough. They will still be expecting and will continue to make demands. I know those kinds of people.'

I want to ask her, *what kind of people*, but I know her

response will get my blood boiling and I am still freaked out at the way I manhandled her a few days ago so I let it slide. Instead I say. 'I want to go back after I finish my exams.'

Ma looks put out by the idea. She says, 'And where will you stay?

'At my father's place.'

'Bobo, Bobo. Life is not as simple as it seems. Your Aunt Jean smiled at you on Friday because you were only there for a day. You land there tomorrow with a big suitcase and watch her expression change. The woman has three children of her own and a sick husband. She doesn't need an extra son to look after.'

'Then I will stay with George. A guy I met in Sempa.'

Ma laughs. 'You're going to live with someone you've only known a day?'

I am trying to keep my cool but I can feel the anger rising in me. Ma is talking to me as if I'm a child who has not thought my plans through. I say to her that she has a point, so I will rent one of the empty workers quarters. I remind her I have four hundred dollars I won in a National Science Innovation Project and I will use the money for food and rent in Sempa. She looks completely surprised because I tell her I have calculated that the money is enough for three weeks rent. One way or another I am going to bond with my other family so she might as well give me her blessings.

Ma is quiet. Then she breathes out, lifts herself off the sofa, and says, 'Take the desktop and let them have it. I have warned you but I guess you have to learn the hard way.' She starts to walk away, then turns around as if she has just remembered something. 'Did you hand in the science project?'

I nod. I know where the conversation is going. 'So who are you going to the dance with on Saturday?'

I start to say I'm undecided but then I remember my promise to be true to myself and not allow myself to be influenced by others. 'I have asked Sula, although she has not replied to my text.'

'The girl from Bellington?'

'Sula.'

'I didn't realise you and Sula had become close. Is it because of the science project? Who matched you up for the project?'

'Brother Paul put us in pairs. She didn't have a partner, I didn't have one so I thought to ask her.'

'Mercy would have gone with you.'

'I've asked Sula.'

'Is she coming? Do you have any idea what she will wear?'

'I'm sure she's got something to wear.'

'Bobo, are you sure you want to invite her or are you doing this to challenge me?'

'Over the past few days I found out my father was nearly dying and I discovered a young brother who looked at me as if I was a god. I saw sick people queuing up in a hospital that has no running water.' I don't add that I also spent the night with a girl of the night, although I wonder what she would do if she knew. 'These things have made me see the world around me differently. And because of this, the dance just seems so trivial in comparison. It's just a few hours of eating and dancing, what does it matter who sits by my side?'

Ma's face loses shape. 'I am so sorry Bobo about all that has happened over the past few days. I wish you didn't have to go through it all. I shouldn't have let you go to Sempa. I wish I could change things.'

'Ma, what happened is life. I had to see it. In fact, thank you for letting me go to Sempa.'

Ma suddenly smiles.

'You see Ma, I appreciate all you have done for me. But it felt great to have Eric and his sisters around me. And I want more of them. That is all I'm asking. Yes I may go to Sempa and hate it this time around. Big deal, I'll come back. Just as I may not enjoy having Sula as my partner at the dance but it's only a few hours, it will pass.'

Ma nods into my face as I speak. Then she hugs me. 'Oh Bobo, my Bobo, you have grown into such a wonderful young man. I have to keep reminding myself you are not a baby anymore.'

'But Ma, you also have to realise I may like Sempa and I may like Sula. Because I am me and at times I may like things different from what you like or want.'

Ma nods again. Tears come to her eyes as she leaves the house. Left alone, I sit down, take a deep breath and remind myself that despite all the fights I have with Ma, if I was given a chance to choose another mother, I would still pick her. She was only being a mother, afraid of losing her only child.

Chapter 13

Sula

Finally, it is the day of the dance. Joyce texts me to say she has arranged for someone called Maureen to come and do my hair and makeup at 5.30 p.m. I call Joyce for some moral support as I feel myself start to falter but she doesn't pick up her phone. She texts to say she can't talk but that everything will be okay. I wish she was able to talk to me. I need to hear her voice.

Bambo is out of town so I don't have to worry about him walking around and sneering at all the preparations. I have arranged to meet Ja at the mall. We finally spoke. He called me to apologise for leaving me to hand in the folder. After the conversation I avoided him. Deep inside I was scared he might change his mind about having me as his partner at the dance so I didn't want to give him any chance for that.

During the exams last week, I snuck into the hall and left immediately afterwards. Even though we have been texting each other I have this feeling in my stomach that Ja and I won't end up at the dance together. I keep imagining myself getting to the mall and Ja doesn't show up. Or that Bambo will pitch up unexpectedly just when I am about to leave and bar me from going. I start to wonder what the night will be like. If only it was just Ja and I but the more I think about spending the evening as an outsider and unaccepted member of the gang the more I wish Amai hadn't stood up to Bambo and insisted that I go to the dance. At least then I wouldn't be feeling so queasy from anxiety.

After lunch I'm washing the dishes and trying to calm myself by singing, when I hear someone at the gate and although there is always someone at the gate this time my heart starts beating. I hear

Amai and Amai Mukulu speaking to someone with alarm in their voices. When I go to see who it is Amai Mukulu tells me that an elderly uncle has been rushed to the hospital. She says she and Amai have to leave for the hospital at once. I feel in my bones that it is the start of things going wrong.

Amai Mukulu must have sensed my anxiety because she tells me not to worry. They arrange for Zafika to spend the night at Amake Miriam's house. Before they set off Maureen arrives to do my hair and makeup. Amai calls the taxi man who is to take me to the mall to confirm that he is coming. Amai Mukulu adds to my anxiety by throwing in a few threats about what she'll do to the taxi man if he doesn't show. She reminds him of her instructions to wait for me at the mall until Ja drops me off. She tells him to stay put and not try and make extra money by taxing while I'm at the dance. She hangs up and gives me another pep talk about how cleverer I am than all the skinny, spoilt girls at my school. 'Remember that Ja could have taken any one of them to the dance but he chose you,' she says.

Finally, the two sisters leave. Maureen talks me through the makeup application. She uses plum lipstick because it suits my tone and it will make my teeth look whiter than an orange tone. She says at night the eye makeup should be more dramatic so she uses black liquid eyeliner which stings my eyes so she has to dab my tears away with a soft sponge. She only allows me to look at myself when she has finished and I almost don't recognise myself in the mirror. I ask Maureen to take some pictures of me because I don't think I will ever in my life look and feel so beautiful.

My euphoria is short-lived because the taxi man calls to say he is on the way and I am back at square one. The butterflies start fluttering in my stomach. What will I talk about with Ja for four hours without chemistry or physics equation to solve or a report to write? What if they all start talking about their houses or their parents' jobs? What will I say about Bambo? I try to call Joyce again to ask her what I should say but her phone is still switched off. Alarm bells go off in my head. Joyce always has her phone on. I hope she is not in trouble again.

I hear a knock at the gate. I go out expecting that the taxi driver has arrived early after Amai Mukulu's threats but I get to the gate and find Joyce's helper, Olipa. She is holding a tearful Letti in her arms and two big suitcases stand either side of her.

'You look great!' Olipa says.

'Why are you here?'

She peers past me into the yard and whispers, 'Is Amai here?'

'What's happened?'

'Sister Joyce has gone to South Africa.' Olipa's words set the world around me spinning. 'She asked me to bring Letti here. She has left a letter for you, one for Amai and one for Bambo.'

'South Africa?'

Olipa kept looking over my shoulder. 'She said she will explain.'

I feel weak in the knees so I hold onto the gate to steady myself. 'She didn't tell me. Why didn't she say goodbye?' I whisper because Olipa's words have drained me of all my energy.

'She said Bambo would not have allowed her to go. And she has nothing to do here because Letti's father said he wants nothing to do with her. She said she will come back with her certificate and she will find a job.' Olipa's words are distant in my ears, even though she is obviously telling the truth but I can't understand why Joyce would go far away, without saying goodbye and why she chose tonight of all nights. The light from the verandah catches the teardrops on Letti's face, although she is now smiling and holding her arms out to me. I reach out for her but Olipa gives me her shoulder and keeps Letti away. 'She'll spoil your dress and makeup,' Olipa says.

Maureen, who has been listening to the conversation, helps Olipa carry the cases into the house while I sit on the verandah because I feel weak. I try to make sense of what Joyce has done. I wonder what she has gone to study and for how long she will be away. Olipa insists she will stay with Letti until I return from the dance and that she will set off the next day for the village where her mother lives. I tell her that she can leave because I will not be going to the dance. Suddenly I'm overcome with a strong urge to laugh and to cry at the same time.

The taxi man arrives and I send Olipa outside to ask him to leave but he follows her back through the gate and says he can't go anywhere because Amai Mukulu has paid him for five hours so he will sit in the car as promised. He joins Olipa and Maureen in persuading me to go to the dance, they say how beautiful I look but I have lost the taste for it. I sit on the couch and Maureen picks up my camera and asks me to smile. I try to smile but instead I start to cry. She panics and kneels by me. 'It's okay, it's okay,' she says rocking me gently.

I explain that without Joyce I will be lost. I tell her that I am so disappointed Joyce didn't tell me she was leaving. At that moment, my phone starts to ring and it is Ja. I watch the phone ringing, then pick it up.

I start to tell him I can't make it. In a strong clear voice I say, 'Sorry Ja. But I have a problem...' that's as far as my strong voice carries. I just about manage the words, 'I can't make it today,' and then I'm crying. I hear him ask me what has happened. But I can't say anything. So I hang up.

Letti is up and crying in the bedroom so I take off my heels and rush to pick her up. I notice her body is very warm and sticky as I carry her back out and sit with her in my lap. Maureen hands me a cloth to stop Letti messing my dress. Though she is just two and feeds herself, I hold her feeding cup for her because I feel some comfort holding her. I tell Maureen to ask the driver to take her home. He agrees but says he will be back because Amai Mukulu will kill him if he doesn't stay by me for the five hours she has paid him for. I sit alone on the chair, and find myself singing *Amazing Grace* to Letti.

I am woken up by the sound of a car horn at the gate. I realise Letti has fallen asleep just as I have. I realise that Joyce has not turned up laughing at me for falling for her joke. The horn goes off again and my heart sinks as I realise Joyce is really gone and I was only dreaming she was back. Before I can stand up Olipa, who has been watching TV inside, rushes past me and out to the gate. I get up to put Letti down on my bed.

As I head back outside I catch a glimpse of myself in the mirror. I twirl around in the mirror and then decide to put my shoes back on. Perhaps Olipa is right, I should take more pictures so Maureen's efforts don't go to waste. I take the camera and go outside. I find Olipa coming back inside, Ja is behind her, sporting a black suit, a crisp white shirt and a red bowtie.

I'm too shocked to say anything. Olipa steps out of the way and Ja and I face each other. I walk back to the verandah. He looks at Letti's empty baby bottle.

'My niece. My sister's daughter.'

'The sister that needs to be kept in check?' Smiling, he pulls a folding chair that is resting against the wall and sits on it. His chair is facing mine. 'You look great.'

I smile, unsure of what to say. He reaches for the camera in my hand. 'May I?'

I swallow the painful lump in my throat and smile, and he

takes a picture. Then he gets up and kneels beside me to show me the image. I see myself smiling sadly, perhaps shyly, perhaps wearily, into the camera.

'Let's take another one.' He puts his arm around me and holds the camera out with the other. The flash goes off in my face. When he shows me the picture we laugh at it. The two of us blinking at the flash. He takes another one. It is much better. Ja sits back in the folding chair.

We are quiet for a while. Someone somewhere is frying fish, the smell of fresh fish in hot oil fills the warm air. I take in our surroundings and wonder what Ja makes of the worn cushion he is sitting on, or the piles of fashion catalogues stacked in the corner of the verandah. I hope he hasn't noticed the crack in the living room window which is covered with sellotape. I think of the glass living room doors in his living room.

'Aren't you late for the dance?' I ask.

'What good is a dance without a partner?'

'I'm sorry. It's just that my sister left tonight without saying goodbye.'

'You aren't doing a good job keeping her in check.'

I smile at his words. 'She asked Olipa the helper to bring her here.'

'Don't worry or try and guess why she didn't say goodbye, wait for her to tell you. Give her a chance to give her side of the story. And by the way we can still dance.' Ja reaches into his pocket and fishes out his iPod. He stands up, holds his hand out to me. When I hesitate he reaches up, takes my hand and pulls me to my feet. He pulls apart the strings of his ear phone, puts one in his ear and hands me the other. I put it in my left ear, then he pulls me closer, and we dance.

'Sula and Ja,' he whispers to me.

When the song ends, Ja looks at his time. 'We have missed the dinner but we can make it to the dance.'

I look at him, unsure what to say.

Ja takes my hand and says, 'Let's go to the dance.'

As I absorb his words, my phone starts to ring. There's no caller ID. I pick up the phone and Joyce says: 'Hi Sula!' She sounds breathless. 'Are you at the dance? Did he come?' I catch myself nodding into the phone, then I realise she can't see me. Before I can open my mouth, she says. 'Listen. I am at the airport. I am going to South Africa to study for a Diploma in travel and tourism management.

'To study?'

'Yes, Sula! Remember what Sister Miriam said? I paid a full year's fees direct to the College and I will stay with my friend June. Remember her? She works as a nurse and she says I can stay with her.'

'What will Amai say?'

'I will write to them. I have to do something for myself to make everyone proud. You can't be a doctor with an elder sister who is a loafer!' I heard her giggle on the other end.

I start to laugh. She also laughs. Then she says she has to go. Before she hangs up she says, 'I am proud of you, baby sister. Enjoy the dance.' And just like that she is gone.

'It's my sister. She called to say goodbye and to ask me to enjoy the dance.'

'So what are we waiting for? Let's go to the dance!'

Mr Mwati who has been sitting in the car outside the gate drives us there. The taxi man follows behind. We get to the centre where the dance is being held and Ja helps me out the car and leads me into the building. We climb up the stairs and find Mr Edwards the history teacher at the door to the Banqueting Hall. Ja explains that that we were held up.

Although we have missed the opening of the floor when all the couples are called to the floor, Mr Edwards asks us to wait outside the hall while he arranges for us to be called in. We stand behind the door until it is opened from the inside and Ja leads me in. He leads me to the centre of the floor.

I feel the eyes on me but I don't look around. This is my moment. I want it to last forever. Ja turns to face me. The names Sula and Ja boom through the speaker, then the music starts.

And we dance, again.

Printed in the United States
By Bookmasters